UG

GC Fabbri

shed9

First published in Stockholm, Sweden 2022
Shed9 AB, Hagagatan 20, 11348, Stockholm, Sweden

ISBN 978-91-988222-0-5

www.shed9.com/ug
www.garyfabbri.com

For Maxi & Ruben
Always

Contents

I've Got a Name

It's not a nickname if only your brothers use it.

They sling it at you when you're alone with them, balled up in the chair, kicking wildly.

'UG.'

They shout it when you're lucky enough to land a shot and knock them back, away from you.

'UG!'

They whisper it when Mom's making dinner and can't hear their voices over the hiss of frying peppers.

'Uuuuuuuuuuuug.'

They don't spell it out, but you know exactly what they mean.

Ug is for ugly.

When they say it, it hurts more than a hundred punches, jabs and pinches. It hurts more than a kick under the table that makes it impossible to drink your milk without spilling it.

It hurts because it doesn't feel like you.

Mom HAS heard them say it. She gives them the evil eye and tells me to ignore them. But how can I ignore them when they use it more than a nickname.

They walk by in the hall, 'Hey, Ug.'

They're going out to play in the snow. 'See you, Ug.'

They're heading out for basketball practice and throw the ball at you, 'Catch, Ug.'

They call me 'Ug', but I wish they wouldn't.

My real name is Rebecca.

Fighting Back

It's not that I don't fight back, because I do.

'You're such a loser, UG,' said Kenny.

'You're the one who struck out on Sunday,' I shot back.

I knew this would set him off. I just couldn't help it. He's always talking about how great he is. Then, at his last baseball game, he struck out with one man on base and his team lost.

I ran to the armchair in the living room. It's my best position because I'm protected from behind and I can use my legs to kick. The chair is perfect because it becomes like a turtle shell. Once I start kicking, I'm like a machine.

I had my shoes on, even though they're not allowed in the house. That makes my kicks count. Kenny came in fast, whacking my thighs. I kicked back hard, but his arms are long and he got a few good shots in.

I kicked wildly and he yanked off one of my shoes. He raised it over my head and I took the chance. Kicked hard again.

Belly shot. He bent over. I could tell it was painful. And I felt bad for an instant. I didn't want to hurt him.

'Leave me alone,' I shouted.

He breathed in deeply. His eyes filled with a kind of angry fire. He lifted the shoe and threw it down at me. A torpedo blast, but I caught it, just in front of my face.

He jumped on top and punched, punched, punched my legs. Then he stood up and looked down at me to see if he could get a better shot in.

I lifted the shoe and threw it at him with all my might, but I missed Kenny and the shoe smashed into the end table lamp. That put an end to the battle for that day.

'Come on,' said David from the doorway. 'Let's get out of here.'

I picked up the pieces while my brothers disappeared outside to play in the backyard.

It was peaceful and quiet when they went out.

That night when Mom got home from work, I told her it was an accident. She said that she was happy that I wasn't hurt by the broken glass.

But you can't go breaking lamps every day to get a little peace.

They both whispered 'Ug!' at me when I went upstairs to bed that night.

Mom heard them and told them to stop. But they never listen to her.

Not Every Second

We don't fight every single second from the moment we get home from school. Sometimes Kenny makes fried apples and I help him.

He loves to make fried apples. They taste like apple pie filling without the crust, all soft and cinnamony.

'You core and I'll slice,' he said.

We worked until we had a mound of thin wedges.

'Let's use Mom's butter,' I suggested.

'Good idea,' he agreed.

Mom doesn't usually let us eat the real butter. She says it's too expensive, so she buys tubs of margarine for us. We tried to fry the apples in the beginning with margarine, but real butter worked better.

I cut wedges of hard butter and slipped them into the pan.

If Mom ever noticed how much butter we use, she hasn't said anything about it.

The apple pieces began to sizzle as he put them in. We added lots of sugar. Two kinds. Granulated and sticky brown. We go through a lot of cinnamon, too, when we make fried apples. It's soooooo good.

Kenny added a few extra chunks of butter into the mix while it was frying.

The amazing smells of holidays filled the air.

I stepped out the back door and took a few breaths of the outside air so that when I came back in again I got a fresh whiff of our frying apples.

The apples became hot and sweet.

When they were done, Kenny was fair divvying them up. Three bowls with equal amounts. He rinsed the pan and washed it before we were allowed to eat. I cleared off the counter.

That was the rule. Clean first, then enjoy.

It's a good rule because it gives the apples just enough time to cool so you can eat them without burning your tongue.

I don't know what David does while we're cooking, but he always appears just when we're ready to eat.

David is good at disappearing when there are chores to do. He's never around when it's time to set the table or do the dishes either. Sometimes I wish I had his knack for disappearing.

'Ok. All set,' said Kenny.

We each grabbed a bowl and went to the living room and put on the TV.

I didn't care what was on. I just wanted my bowl of apples to last as long as possible.

Fried apple days are good days.

Medium

I am not ugly.

At least not so ugly that people turn their heads on the street when I walk past. If I stand in line to buy a movie ticket, other kids don't move away from me.

I would say that I am medium.

Height – medium.

Weight - medium.

Hair - medium dark brown.

Skin - medium.

Stink - medium. And not at all stinky when you compare me to lots of boys in my class.

I'd say that if you didn't know me, then you wouldn't notice me and I kind of like it that way … I think. People have said that I'm a tomboy, but I don't feel like a tomboy. Not exactly. I'm just not too girly.

I'm a pretty good runner. My legs are strong. I suppose it comes from all of that after-school kicking.

There aren't too many boys in my class who are faster.

I never give up.

My Mom has said that I'm the most stubborn person she knows.

She doesn't mean it as a compliment, but I think it's one of my best features.

I like being stubborn because I get stuck into things. And once I get stuck, I can go on forever, even if it hurts.

Mom says that I don't listen.

But I do listen. I just tend to ignore most of what Mom says because she spends like eighty percent of her time defending the boys.

When you're medium you don't stick out and you don't get picked on at school.

Boy Friend

My brothers don't call me UG at school because I've gotten good at avoiding them.

It's pretty easy because …

a. They're older. Kenny by two years and David by one.

b. They don't want any of their friends to see me with them.

So no one hears them call me that.

The biggest problem that I have at school is that my best friend is a boy. I think that the fact that he has a girl as a best friend is a bigger problem for him. But there's nothing either one of us can do about it.

And there's nothing 'boyfriend' or 'girlfriend' about our friendship. It started when I walked into history class with Mr. McCartney at the beginning of the year. He teamed me up with Lorenzo and we became friends right away.

Lorenzo's from Italy. He was actually born there and moved to America when he was three, so he doesn't have an accent or anything.

His dad has a huge Italian accent.

Lorenzo's mom speaks English with an English accent, even though she's Italian too. It's also funny to hear, but way easier to understand. He has a little brother Marco who is just a baby. Marco is so cute!

Lorenzo's mom let me hold Marco the other day and she said that some day when I was older, I could babysit! That would be so cool. I would love to babysit little Marco.

I asked mom if I could go over to Lorenzo's after school instead of coming home, but she said 'NO.'

When I asked her why not she said, 'because I said so.'

'Because I said so,' isn't a good reason, but I couldn't get her to give me a better one even though I cried and screamed until supper time.

I don't want Lorenzo to come home with me after school when Mom's not at home because I'm pretty sure my brothers would beat on him too and he's not as good a fighter as me, so he would be crushed.

But I can go over there on weekends once my mom is up and sometimes Lorenzo comes to our house. My mom is really nice when other kids come over. She makes cookies and talks a lot and smiles. She does that even when Kenny and David have friends over.

My brothers have lots of activities on the weekends and that keeps her busy, running around. I have some too. I street dance and I play soccer. I'm not the best dancer, but I'm pretty good at soccer, though. My speed and stubbornness help me on the field.

And I've learned lots since I started practicing with Lorenzo in his back yard. His dad is awesome. When he has time on Saturdays, he teaches us all kinds of tricks. He says that in Italy everyone plays soccer better than anyone in America. But they call it 'calcio' there. Lorenzo's mom says that they call it football in England and everywhere else in the world except for America.

Lorenzo's dad says why do they call American football 'football' when they hardly use their feet? He waves his hand in front of his face. 'I cannota understanda!' It makes me giggle.

Lorenzo plays soccer too, but on a different team. He plays on a boys' team in a regional league. You have to try out to get in. Lorenzo's dad is the coach.

Some Saturdays we both play soccer in different places so we don't have time to meet up.

Lorenzo's dad watches us practice together and says that I have a natural talent and that if I work hard I could be really good. That makes my stubborn streak kick in. I really want to be good at something.

He says, 'the boys in America, they are no good at a football. But the girls, they are best in the world.'

Imagine being best in the world!

Calling Mom

Mom works.

I call her sometimes, but it's like calling the wall. She has to work.

If I manage to get her on the phone, she hears us screaming. Then she shouts back, 'you have to stop fighting, Rebecca! I don't want you fighting. Do you understand me! Put your brother on!'

I hand the phone to either of them and Mom uses her stern voice in the background. 'Leave your sister alone!'

'It wasn't me! She was kicking!'

Then I shout, 'you started it!'

Because they always do. I don't want to fight. I have to fight.

Mom shouts down the phone. 'I'm at work! You need to stop or there's going to be hell to pay when I get home.'

So, I don't say anything else. 'Hell to pay,' sounds worse than kicking to me. I don't think my brothers like the idea of 'hell to pay' either so they usually hang up and stalk off.

'See you, Ug!'

'Wouldn't want to be you, Ug!'

When I hear the bounce of their basketball in the backyard, I'm safe.

As long as the basketball continues to bang, slap and ding against the rim, I'm free to read.

The armchair in the living room isn't only a great place to fight from, it's also a great place to sink into with a book.

It feels like it wraps its soft warm green arms around me as I read. A standing lamp with an orange plastic shade hangs over my head and sheds a warm glow down on me.

I can disappear into that chair and stay there while the sound of the basketball slips further into the distance, but it's important that I can still hear it. For me the bang, slap and ding, beat out the rhythm of freedom.

The liberation of that bouncing ball allows the words that I read to weave through the page like Pelé passing defenders. It's like running on a clear, open field.

If the rhythmic basketball beat is broken, then it's time for defense. It means I only have a few moments before they take charge on the offensive …

'What are you doing, Ug?'

'Catch, Ug!'

Basketballs are hard.

'You're uglier than my butt hole, Ug!'

'Yeah. You're butt ugly.'

I sink in deeper. Legs cocked. I'm ready for battle.

'Ug!'

Number Zero

Bad news.

I could see it the second she came in, but she waited until dinner to dish it out.

'I'm sorry Rebecca, but you're going to have to quit the soccer team.'

There it was, like a side order of soggy peas. Why do parents even dish out peas to begin with?

'What? Why?'

'It clashes with the boys' baseball practice.'

'I can give up dance instead.'

'But that won't change anything because dance is on Sundays and that doesn't clash with baseball.'

'Why is their baseball more important than my soccer?!' I shouted.

Then Kenny said, 'everyone knows that baseball is more important than soccer … especially girls' soccer.'

'That's because American boys suck at soccer!' I shouted.

'What did you say?!' asked Mom.

'You heard me, they suck!'

I knew that would get me in trouble, but I didn't care.

'I don't want you talking like that,' said Mom.

'I'm playing!'

'No, I'm sorry Rebecca. We'll find something else for you. There are other activities that don't clash.'

'I don't want to do other activities. I want to play football!' I shouted it the European way.

'Football!' said Kenny. 'Now she wants to play football. Ha! Girls playing football.'

'You're so dumb!' I shouted. 'That's what the rest of the world calls it. Football, not soccer. Or calcio in Italy!'

'Well, we don't live in the rest of the world,' said Kenny.

'I want you to stay out of this Kenny,' said Mom.

'Ok. I'll leave you with UG!'

'Kenny,' said Mom.

He just sauntered off. He called me UG right in front of her and all she said was 'Kenny.'

'I'm not quitting,' I said.

'Can't you do an extra school activity on a weekday?'

'When they want to do something, it's fine. But when I want to do something, you just don't care.'

'I do care, but we can't do it. Besides, they both play baseball together, so we can go together. You can just come with me we could …'

Then she paused for a long moment.

'Watch,' she said.

'You want me to WATCH them play baseball?!'

'Yes, it could be our time. Just you and me.'

'Sitting on the sidelines?'

'Don't see it that way. You like reading. We could read together.'

I was getting nowhere. So I tried to change my tactics. 'Can't I play football? Please. Maybe I can get a ride with someone or something.'

'You like soccer now,' she said. 'But you'll forget all about it after a week.'

'I won't forget!'

'You will.'

'I'm playing football.'

'No, I'm sorry, Rebecca.'

'Why are you against football?' What has it done to you?'

'It's soccer, Rebecca. And I'm not against it. I just think that Saturdays are too packed with other things right now. And it would be good for us to spend time together.'

'Good for you!' I shouted.

'No. Good for all of us.'

'You don't know anything about what's good for me!'

'I do, Rebecca.'

'If you knew, then Dad would still be here.'

'Rebecca,' she said. Her lip trembled. 'This has nothing to do with me and your father.'

'It has everything to do with him. You think you can decide. You think you know what's best for everyone. But you don't! He couldn't stand you, so he left!'

'It's not like that, Rebecca.'

'You think you know, but you don't know anything!'

'I know this, you're not playing soccer and that's final.'

'I hate you!' I shouted and I ran up to my room, but it didn't do me any good.

Mom never came up.

I could hear her downstairs. The TV was on. She was probably watching some sitcom with Kenny and David. Laughing.

My heart pounded. I pulled my hair. Hard. Harder.

I wanted to cry but I wasn't crying. I pulled so hard that my scalp burned but my tears were trapped.

'Football,' I said. 'Football. I love football.'

I knew. I was going to play … NO … MATTER … WHAT!!!

At that same moment tears exploded from my eyes.

I wanted to cry but I wasn't crying. I pulled so hard that my scalp burned but my tears were trapped.

'Football,' I said. 'Football. I love football.'

I knew. I was going to play … NO … MATTER … WHAT!!!

At that same moment tears exploded from my eyes.

The Silent Treatment

We weren't speaking.

At least I wasn't. Mom acted like she was nice this morning. 'What would you like for breakfast, Rebecca?'

She never made breakfast on weekdays. I always ate the same thing. A bowl of cereal with frozen blueberries and milk. I love the way the blueberries get a thin white coating as soon as you drop them into the milk and I eat a few of them first before they start to soften.

Mom does make breakfast sometimes on Sundays … when the boys don't have practice. But only Sundays. And it's always the same thing. Pancakes with maple syrup and small Brown n' Serve sausages because Kenny and David love them.

I think they're a bit like peppery rubber sticks, but I love pancakes. Who doesn't?

'What are you doing at school today, Rebecca?'

What a lame question. Whenever Mom's trying to pretend to be nice, she always asks lame questions. If she had asked me a real question, like 'why do you want to play soccer so badly?' I might have answered. But as it was, I didn't say a single word.

'Rebecca, please, say something.'

She hated the silent treatment. It was my best weapon against her.

But today it didn't work.

'Ok, suit yourself,' she said. 'Boys, come down for breakfast,' she called.

I was actually glad to see them because I didn't have to listen to her pretend to be nice to me anymore.

I finished my cereal, rinsed my bowl, grabbed my bag and my soccer ball and left the house for the bus stop without saying another word.

I was the first one there. My brothers would be along in a while, but I could practice until then. I bounced the ball on my right knee first, then left, then toe, toe. I aimed for the rhythm. Right, left, toe, toe, right left, toe, toe. Lorenzo was brilliant at juggling the ball and could keep going without it hitting the ground for the longest time.

I was getting better at juggling. But the thing that I was best at was that I was strong and could kick the ball hard. Lorenzo's dad said that I was a perfect wing. I like the idea of being a wing. I can fly.

Mom came out with my brothers. That was unusual. Normally, she would just hop in the car and leave when we waited for the bus.

I was in mid-juggle when she said, 'Rebecca!'

The ball shot out from my toe, zipping out into the street.

Some neighbor that I didn't know screeched her car to a halt. The ball shot across the hood, bounced off the steps of Mr. Walker's across the street, flew up into the air, bounced on the top of the roof of the car right towards Mom's head.

David reached out and snatched it from in front of her nose and spun it on his finger like a basketball.

The woman in the car rolled down her window. 'You should tell your kids not to play ball in the streets!'

'I apologize,' said Mom. 'They know it's not allowed.'

She glared at me with evil Mom eyes. I raised my backpack over my face to deflect them.

'Rebecca!' she said.

I maintained my vow of silence.

'Rebecca!'

The woman in the car shouted, 'you should have better control of your kids.'

I was glad for that because Mom turned her attention to the woman, 'do you have anything else to say? Do you want to file a police report or something?!'

'Well, I just might,' puffed the woman.

'Well you just go right ahead. Do it or drive on!' shouted Mom.

The woman said, 'you're lucky there was no damage.'

Mom said, 'you'd better move along or maybe there will be some!'

The woman huffed and gunned her engine.

I smiled to myself and kind of respected Mom for a moment. I was about to break the silent treatment when she turned to David and plucked the spinning ball from his finger.

She wrapped her arms around it and laser blasted a look at me. 'You see this ball …' She stuck her finger in it like she was trying to pop a balloon.

Of course, it wasn't going to pop. It was a professional FIFA approved, hand-sewn football made to withstand a kick from the best players in the world. My mom's fingernail couldn't scratch it.

'I'm taking this with me and I don't want to see you with a soccer ball again. Do you hear me young lady?!'

I wasn't talking. And I certainly wasn't a lady!

'I'm talking to you!'

If I were talking to her, I would have said 'talk to the hand!' But I didn't say a word. I just hugged my backpack and thought, if I take one step closer, I can kick that thing right out from under her arm. And there'd be nothing she could do about it.

I watched her walk back towards the driveway. She opened the door of the car, threw the ball in the back seat, crawled in and slammed the door. She revved the engine. The flesh in her cheeks shook as she popped the car into reverse. I could see her teeth clenched as she backed out of the drive.

She drove past, as if in slow motion, taking my soccer ball with her. It felt like she was taking my cat to the vet to have him put down.

I hated her.

My brothers were silent too. I knew they saw the tears on my cheeks. One word out of them and I would have kicked their teeth in. I would have kicked until my legs were sore.

The bus rolled around the corner and stopped in front of us.

We climbed on and my brothers disappeared towards the back. I sat in the front clutching my backpack, hoping no one would notice me.

Silent.

I wanted to cry but I wasn't crying. I pulled so hard that my scalp burned but my tears were trapped.

'Football,' I said. 'Football. I love football.'

I knew. I was going to play … NO … MATTER … WHAT!!!

At that same moment tears exploded from my eyes.

My Favorite Class

History.

A lot of people think that history is boring. They think that it's all about memorizing a lot of facts or old things that don't matter anymore. But I don't.

Mr. McCartney stood in front of the class and raised one finger into the air, 'history isn't true,' he said. Then he gave us that strange mysterious look he does by raising one eyebrow high up on his forehead.

A lot of people don't think you can change history. They think that once something has happened then that's it. But I don't think it works exactly that way.

Then Mr. McCartney said, 'people have changed history, throughout history.' And his eyebrows switched sides.

'Why do I say that?' he asked but he didn't expect an answer.

'Think of history as stories. Historians change history by writing it down. Because as soon as you write something down it turns into a story.'

'You can't write everything down, can you? When you write something, even a list of (so called) facts, you leave a lot to people's imagination.'

'When you write things down, you also leave out a lot of real stuff. Go ahead and try to write down everything you see, for one day. You can't do it.'

'Sounds boring anyway,' said one of the boys in the back.

'Shhhhhh … boring,' said Mr. McCartney. 'Lists of facts are, in fact, boring. But why?' This time he raised both eyebrows, 'because lists don't carry stories. And good stories are never boring.'

'When you look at old pictures, you kind of think that everything used to be black and white. But there were just as many colors in Benjamin Franklin's day? Hard to believe, isn't it?'

'Even one word has so many meanings and interpretations that you can't paint the complete picture of what actually happened with them.' Mr. McCartney looked around the classroom. 'There's a famous story of three blind men who come across an elephant. Each of them is asked to describe the elephant afterwards. The first of them says, 'it is like a long snake.' The second says 'an elephant is like a mighty wall.' The third one says, 'it is like the trunk of an ancient tree.' Which of them is right?

Donna raised her hand first. She always raises her hand first. And though I think Mr. McCartney is excellent in almost every other way, he always picks her first too.

'Donna?'

'All of them, Mr. McCartney.'

'Exactly. All of them. Because all three blind men feel different parts of the elephant. The first one feels the trunk, the second the body and the third, the leg.'

'But if they could see, they'd know it was an elephant,' said Donna.

'True, but would they see the same elephant? If they were going to describe an elephant, would it look exactly the same to all of them? This is the same thing with history. If I say the word 'elephant' you each get a picture of an elephant based on another picture of an elephant. Most of us have been to the zoo and seen an elephant up close. What did you notice when you saw the elephant at the zoo?'

'The way it smelled,' blurted out Lorenzo.

'Yes! Good! The word elephant or a picture of an elephant can't describe the smell of an elephant. What else?'

'The way it swayed its head,' I said.

'Yes! It swayed and moved. You see, once you start exploring a single word … elephant … a story begins. And that story is both the elephant's story and the reader's story. The way that you describe something that happened would be totally different from the way I describe it. And the way that you read something is totally different from the way that I read it.'

'Now, think for a moment, of your own story …'

'Boring …' moaned Brian Feeney from the back.

'That's a shame,' said Mr. McCartney. 'Imagine, you write your own story and you write … Boring,' Mr. McCartney wrote the word on the chalkboard. 'There it is … is that really your story? If you don't want your story to be boring, change it. When you change your story, you change history!'

'Now, I want you to pick something that you're interested in. It could be a sport or an activity, but something that you like to do and write a short history of it.'

Mr. McCartney turned to the class.

'Brian. What do you like to do?'

Brian Feeney reminded me of my brother, Kenny. I hoped he didn't have a little sister.

'I like to play video games,' he said.

'Good. You can write a history of video games. I look forward to learning about them.'

Tommy Rainer raised his hand so high that he practically jumped out of his seat.

'Tommy?'

'I like to watch TV.'

'Great. What do you like to watch?'

'Ahhhh, cartoons.'

'Excellent. A history of the cartoon.'

Lots of kids picked different types of TV programs and movies. Donna picked ballet. John Rockwell picked the boy scouts.

'Rebecca?' said Mr. McCartney.

'Soccer,' I said.

'Soccer, The Beautiful Game,' said Mr. McCartney. 'What a brilliant idea!'

I didn't know what he meant by The Beautiful Game, but I would find out.

'What about you, Lorenzo?'

Lorenzo looked around the room. He seemed lost. He didn't do anything but go to school, play soccer and hang around with me. Mr. McCartney smiled.

I had a strange feeling, almost like he was saying that it was ok to ask, so I did.

'Can Lorenzo and I work on soccer together?' I asked.

'Is that something that you'd like to do, Lorenzo?' asked Mr. McCartney.

'Yes, please,' said Lorenzo.

'Well, it's your story. You two can be the soccer team.'

I couldn't wait.

Mr. McCartney dismissed the class.

Before we stood up to leave, I opened my notebook and scribbled a few notes to get us started. 'Soccer, football, calcio, The Beautiful Game.' Not boring.

Saturday

Mom liked to sleep late on Saturday mornings.

If I bothered her, she would either get really angry or she would say 'yes' to almost anything to get rid of me quickly.

There was also a possibility that she may get angry AND say yes, but either way there was a good chance of a YES before 8am on Saturday.

If I waited until she was fully awake, I could never predict what she would say. I didn't want to risk a NO.

I couldn't stand the idea of sitting around the house all day, alone. Even worse would be following Mom and my brothers to baseball practice while I missed soccer.

A sleepy 'yes' or an angry 'yes' are still both YESSES.

I slipped into her room.

'Mom,' I whispered.

It was completely silent. The shades were drawn. It smelled nice in Mom's room. She had wall-to-wall carpeting and a big heavy duvet that dampened the sound. There were always clothes scattered about as well.

I never understood how she could get mad about our rooms being messy when hers was always full of clothes she hadn't put away.

'Mom,' I whispered a bit louder.

I walked closer to her bed. It was a high bed, the kind of bed you had to climb up onto.

When Mom was awake, she was pretty. Prettier than me. She had jet black hair and soft pale skin. People told her that she looked a bit like Elizabeth Taylor, who was a famous actress a long, long time ago. Mom would bat her eyelashes at that. Elizabeth Taylor was better than medium, even though she got fat when she was old.

Once Mom and I watched 'National Velvet,' starring Elizabeth Taylor when she was twelve. If that's what Mom looked like when she was my age, then she'd easily be one of the prettiest girls in class. But she'd have to do something about her hair.

But now … when Mom was sleeping she looked more like a zombie than any kind of actress. Her hair shot off in all directions forming a black halo around her head. Her mouth hung open and you could see drool on her cheek. Plus her eyelashes were a lot smaller without her mascara.

I don't know how I look when I'm asleep, but I can't possibly look as different from my awake self as Mom does. It's almost like she's two different people sharing the same body. When Mom's getting ready for work, she sometimes says that she has to 'put her face on.' That is EXACTLY what she does.

'Mom,' I said. I touched her arm.

'Yeah,' she croaked softly.

'Can I go to Lorenzo's?'

'What time is it?'

I needed to get to 'Yes' quickly.

'It's nearly eight. His mom said it was ok with her if it was ok with tarts?' I said to David.

'What?' He said looking up.

'Pop Tarts? Strawberry?'

'Yeah, sure.'

I tossed them to him.

'Thanks,' he said.

'No problem,' I said. 'I'm off to Lorenzo's if mom's looking for me.'

He nodded and tore into the packet. He usually ate them cold. I thought they were better cold too. If you heat them, then you have to juggle them until they're cool again anyway.

I headed for the stairs. There were three ways out of the house. You could use the front door where only guests came in. We weren't allowed to use that, not because it was so nice or fancy or anything, but because if you came in the front, you were right in the living room. If you had mud on your feet, it would instantly be all over the house. The backdoor led to the back yard and then you could go through the gate to get out.

But we usually used the basement door, because there was a spot down there where we kept our backpacks and jackets and things. Each of us had our own hook, including Mom. There was an extra hook that Dad had used when he lived with us but Mom took it over when he moved out and piled it with her own jackets.

Dad never came back once he left. Not even for a visit or for Christmas or anything. Mom said he moved to New Orleans. To be honest, I've kind of forgotten what he looks like. I was only three and a half when he left and Mom threw out nearly all the pictures of him. But I kept one … in my sock drawer. I haven't pulled it out in a while.

I only remember to look at it when I'm out of socks. That doesn't happen too often anymore because Mom lets me do my own laundry now. You might think doing your own laundry is a chore, but it's way more of a chore to have to wear dirty clothes to school because someone else didn't wash them for you. Since I took over my washing, my clothes are always clean and my sock drawer is always full.

My soccer gear was in my gym bag hanging on my hook in the basement. I lifted it off and looped it over my shoulder. I didn't know where Mom had hidden my ball, but Lorenzo had loads of them.

I could still see her poking it with her red fingernail, as if she could do it damage. It made me laugh to myself.

I closed the door gently instead of slamming it like usual, just in case Mom heard and woke suddenly. I like being out in the early morning before other people wake up. Sure, it wasn't that early but kids never went out early on weekends.

I headed up the hill towards Lorenzo's.

Lorenzo's Mom was up with Marco and she opened the door as I approached the steps. 'Rebecca, ciao!' Then she said something in Italian that I didn't understand, but it made me feel wonderful.

'Come in,' she said. 'I was just about to give Marco some cereal. Maybe you want to help me?'

'Yes, please.'

She bounced her way back towards the kitchen with Marco in her arms and placed him in a highchair with a little plastic table built in.

He gripped my finger and we played with some of the toys on the table until the cereal was done. It was a soupy cream of wheat with apricot jam mixed in.

Lorenzo's mom handed me the bowl and a plastic spoon. I loved feeding Marco. He would grab my hand and push it away or pull it forward if he was ready for another bite. If we missed his mouth, I would use the spoon to scoop up what had stuck to his cheek and try again. Lorenzo's mom had taught me that.

I fed Marco while his mom cooked something that smelled delicious.

She set the table with plates for all of us.

Lorenzo came down from his room. 'Hi, Rebecca,' he said in a sleepy voice.

Lorenzo's dad came into the kitchen, 'Buon Giorno, Rebecca! Come stai?' When he said my name, he held the 'e' before the 'cca.' It was almost like he was singing my name.

'Bene,' I said.

'Bene! Bene! Bene!' said Lorenzo's dad. 'You're Italian is getting better and better!'

Lorenzo's mom brought out a great heaping stack of french toast and we all tucked in.

Match

Lorenzo and I sat in the back of the car passing the soccer ball back and forth. He was dressed in his match gear. I was wearing my sweats and hoodie, as usual.

His father drove. It was an away game and it had started to rain.

Lorenzo's dad kept looking at his phone, saying, 'Ojojojojojojoj.'

'What's up, Dad?' asked Lorenzo.

'Some of the players on the team can't come. I don't know if we have enough for a match. And the team that we are playing against, they are tough.'

'Who's canceled?' asked Lorenzo.

'Rafaelo and Michelangelo's parents called this morning and now I got two text messages that Marko and Luigi can't make it either. We need at least nine or we forfeit the game.'

Lorenzo's dad made Italian versions of everyone on the team's name. It was kind of funny. Ralph and Mike became Rafaelo and Michelangelo.

The field was at the edge of a park. Woods ran along the backside. We parked in a gravel lot in front of the field.

The rain fell softly but steadily.

'This is it,' he said.

Lorenzo and I jumped out of the car and ran to the field. He threw the ball in the air and booted it. I ran full steam, pulled it down under control and shot it into the goal.

We passed the ball and a few of Lorenzo's teammates ran onto the field. We all warmed up together. When it rains, it's important to keep moving so you don't stiffen up.

The home team coach was a short, quick-moving, dark man with stubbly whiskers. His team was called the Wild Cats and he seemed like the right coach for them. It looked like two, or maybe even three, of the players on his team were his sons. He called everyone onto the field and spoke loudly.

'I guess the rain kept your players at home today,' he said.

I counted our team. Lorenzo, Pietro, Karl, Martin, Paul, Little Mario, Aldo and Rick … Only eight. I carried the ball.

'You need nine to play. If you don't have them, we'll call it.'

Lorenzo's dad scanned the group. I could see him counting them up. He looked at me and I saw a quick glimmer in his eye … It said to me … 'as if.'

'I can play,' I said.

'There! Nine,' said Lorenzo's dad. 'We have nine.'

'This is a boys' league,' said the Wild Cat coach.

'That's perfect,' said Lorenzo's dad.'

'You mean to tell me, that that's a boy. With the long hair and the purple hoodie?'

Lorenzo's dad tried to ignore the question. 'Ok, let's go,' he said. 'Warm up.'

'What's your name?' asked the Wild Cat coach.

I looked up at him.

This was my chance.

I said the first thing that came to mind.

'They call me UG,' I said.

'UG? What kind of name is that?' asked the coach.

'Italian,' said Lorenzo's dad. We have nicknames for everyone. You've seen the movies. Jimmy Two Eyes, Stefano the Striker, David the Defender. You heard right … This is the UG.'

'Ok, looks like we've got a game, then,' said the coach.

We walked, side-by-side, to our bench and huddled around Lorenzo's dad. Everyone on the team knew me as Rebecca. I'd practiced with them loads of times. But this was my first match.

'Ok, allora!' said Lorenzo's dad. 'Everyone … first. From now on, this is UG. Ok?'

'Yes, coach,' said the group of boys in unison.

'Little Mario. You're going to play goal today?'

'Yeah,' said Little Mario.

'I have the goalie jersey here. Can you loan UG your game jersey for today?'

'Sure coach,' Little Mario peeled off his jersey. He had a white muscle t-shirt under. It looked funny on him because of his long skinny arms. But he handed me his game jersey and Lorenzo's dad gave him the long black and green goalie top.

I took off my hoodie and slipped Little Mario's jersey over my t-shirt. All the boys watched me. It was like they never saw a person put on a game jersey before. But as soon as I pulled it down, I felt like I became one of them and they turned their eyes back to Lorenzo's dad.

'Ok, this team that we're playing is tough. They won the regional championship last year. Very focused. They play like brothers. This is good but it's also a weakness. It's going to be a long game. We've got no one on the bench so you'll be in there the whole time. It's wet. We have to pass a lot. We create speed through passing, not by running.'

'The ball moves faster when you kick it, than when you babysit it all the way forward. Eh? Control, pass, run. Get in position. Pass again. Shoot. Goal. That's how we win.'

'Ok, let's go.'

I was on the left, mid-field wing. Nervous. Pietro and Lorenzo played forward. The first time the ball came to me I fumbled and one of the three brothers from the other team was on me. He stole the ball and shot down the field.

I could feel the red glow in my cheeks.

Lorenzo's dad shouted, 'Run UG, run!'

It was like waking from a dream. I looked at him and then turned and saw the ball disappearing behind me. I turned back and bee-lined for the middle of the field. One of the brothers tried to break through the center, but Paul and Karl shut him down.

He tried to pass out towards the sideline and I intercepted. By the time I turned and faced up field, I had another guy in my face. I wasn't waiting this time. I kicked across the field, passing to Pietro. It wasn't a good pass. It was too high and hard, but he headed it down and started to run forward. Lorenzo swung round and the two of them were on the attack.

The other team's defenders clamped down on them hard.

Lorenzo passed back to Pietro, who took a shot, but the goalie made an easy save.

I was now playing soccer. In my first match ... with boys.

I was in the right place at the right time. Exactly where I should be.

Thank God it was raining so no one could see the tears running down my cheeks. I was crying but I wasn't going to stop running.

The next time I ran for the ball I made a quick, straight pass to Pietro, who drove forward again. Lorenzo sprinted for a pass. The ball shot behind Lorenzo and I picked it up. Aldo ran up the middle. I passed back to him and he shot. A hard, strong kick. It hit the post and bounced off.

I ran for the ball, with my cleats gripping the mud.

I was in the middle of my first Beautiful Game.

Drenched

We didn't win.

We were totally drenched. Even Lorenzo's dad was soaked through. The rain had increased during the match and most of the parents who were watching had retreated to their cars. They ran their windshield wipers to try to keep track of the game.

Lorenzo's dad called the team together. 'We didn't win today. But we played well. There's no shame in losing when you play well. We could have used a few extra fresh players but that's the way it goes sometimes. We passed well, we made some good attacks and most important - we have a new team member. Rebecca, if you'd like you can join the team as a full-time member. Right boys?'

'Yeah! You played great,' said Pietro. 'Good passing.'

'Excellent,' said Lorenzo.

'You can really move the ball,' said Aldo.

'Can I have my jersey back, though,' said Little Mario.

'Of course,' I said. I peeled it off and felt the cold rain for the first time. I pulled my hoodie from my bag. It was soaked through, but I didn't care.

'Ok, Rebecca, Welcome to the team!' said Lorenzo's dad.

'Call me UG,' I said, and I meant it.

'Ok UG. You're in.'

Everyone reached their arms in. 'Uno, due, tre … this is our day!'

We walked towards the car in the rain. We were parked next to the Wild Cat Coach's car. His three boys climbed into the back. They chattered about the win. Lorenzo walked beside me.

Lorenzo's dad nodded to the Wild Cat Coach, 'Good match, Coach,' he said. 'It was a good win.'

'Thanks Emilio,' he said.

It was the first time I'd heard Lorenzo's dad's name.

The Wild Cat Coach motioned with his head towards me. 'It's a good mid-fielder you've found there,' he said. 'Hope you can keep HIM.'

I knew then that he was sure that I was a girl, but I couldn't tell if he was being nice or if he was threatening to tell someone.

'Everything works out the way it should,' said Lorenzo's dad.

'Ha, Emilio, you're a philosopher. Too bad that doesn't help you on the field.'

'Ok, Coach,' said Lorenzo's dad. Enjoy the rain.'

We got in the car.

Lorenzo sat in silence. I'd never seen him like that.

'What's up Lorenzino?' said Lorenzo's dad, looking in the rearview mirror.

'I missed two good chances. Wide open shots. It should have been a tie.'

I knew what he was talking about because I had passed them to him, right by one of the pillar defenders.

'Hey, it was raining. We were the visiting team.'

'That's no excuse,' said Lorenzo.

'You know, the best players in the world miss sometimes. It happens,' said Lorenzo's dad. 'Sometimes there's no reason.'

'But there is a reason,' said Lorenzo. 'I know why I missed.'

'Why is that, Lorenzino?'

'I missed because I was surprised. I didn't expect to get such good passes. It's my fault, Rebecca. I should have turned those two passes into goals.'

'It's ok,' I said.

'I'm sorry,' he said.

'It's ok,' I said. 'It was the best game ever!'

'But we lost because of me.'

'Not to me,' I said. 'To me, we won. I didn't even expect to play, so how could you expect me to pass to you?'

He looked at me and smiled.

'So perfectly,' I smiled back. 'I mean a second grader could have made those shots with such awesome passing!'

'A kindergartener could have made it,' said Lorenzo.

'Bambino Marco would have made those two goals,' said Lorenzo's dad. 'With his bottle in his mouth!'

Lorenzo's dad pretended that he was sucking a baby bottle.

We all laughed.

I didn't feel wet or cold until Lorenzo's dad pulled in front of our house. I grabbed my bag and climbed out into the rain. It lashed down now. I ran for the door.

Lorenzo called, 'see you Monday!'

I turned and waved as the car pulled away then I went inside.

I could hear the television upstairs. It would soon be supper time. I couldn't go upstairs in my soccer clothes. I pulled off my socks and shin guards. I slid out of my shorts and tore off my hoodie. The washing machine was full of clothes that had not been transferred to the dryer.

I pulled them out and started to put them in the dryer. They smelled slightly sour. Mom must have left them in overnight and all day today.

I stuffed them in the dryer anyway. Maybe the heat would dry away the smell.

I put my clothes in the wash, measured the right amount of detergent, and started the machine.

Standing nude in the basement, all of my dry clothes were up in my room. I couldn't just go up the way that I was. There was no way that I could sneak by my brothers. You had to walk right through the living room to get to the stairs.

I opened the closet where we kept the winter jackets. I saw a big old windbreaker. It could have even been my dad's. I wasn't sure. I wrapped it around myself and headed for the stairs.

I had to climb over Kenny and David's baseball gear lying on the floor in the doorway.

Their baseball clothes were piled up at the bottom of the last step and would probably still be in a stinky clump next Saturday when they had a match again.

If I had seen them before, I would have put them in with my football clothes.

But the washing machine was still filling up, so I picked up the striped wet clump of jerseys and trousers, shook out the mud, and tossed them into the washing machine with my stuff.

I rustled up the stairs in the oversized windbreaker.

Mom was in the kitchen. Saturday night. Beans and hot dogs. She didn't turn, 'Hi, Rebecca. Did you have a nice day at Lorenzo's?'

'Yeah,' I said.

'What'd you get up to in all this rain?'

'Oh. Nothing,' I said.

'Supper's in ten minutes.'

'Ok. I said.'

I walked through the kitchen into the living room. The boys were watching a film.

David looked up at me. 'Nice jacket,' he said.

'Yeah, UG,' said Kenny.

That's me, I thought. 'UG.'

Short

'This has to stop!' Mom's voice reverberated from her desk at work, down the phone and into the kitchen where the receiver lay on the floor.

I had been on the phone with her a moment before when David rounded the corner, pulled a wad of wet paper from his mouth and then rubbed it into my face. I launched a blasting kick that left him wriggling on the floor and dove for the safety of the armchair. From my position, I could hear Mom shouting through the phone.

David hopped up and mounted an attack. He kept pounding into my legs.

'Stop this right now!' I heard Mom's thin voice.

David shouted, 'You kicked me in the nuggets. I'll kill you!' He pummeled my legs like a cartoon character with spinning arms.

It's true. I had landed a nugget shot a moment before. It sent him flying back towards the TV. But it didn't keep him down for long. I dug in hard, ready for retribution.

To be fair, I was aiming for his chin, so it must have been a pretty hard kick. I was standing at the time and had just called Mom because he and Kenny were spitting spitballs at me. My hair was covered in spit paper. It was gross.

I didn't know what happened to Kenny. Maybe he got distracted, or maybe he was busy making the biggest spitball ever.

'I'll kill you, kill you, kill you, kill you!' Each 'kill' was a right cross and each 'you' was a left.

He kept saying it as he punched. I quickly got the rhythm and found a space between a 'kill' and a 'you.' It was like booting the ball away from an attacking player. My legs pulled back and I thrust. David flew off.

It was my second good shot of the day.

All the soccer practice was making me stronger and faster.

I seized the moment and lunged for the phone. I picked it up. Mom was screaming now. 'Stop!'

'Mom!'

'Rebecca!'

'David's punching me.'

David grabbed the phone, 'Mom! She kicked me!'

I heard her voice, 'Give the phone to your sister!'

He threw it at me. 'You're in trouble now!'

I held the phone to my ear. 'What's going on?! Is that right?!'

'He covered my hair in spitballs!'

Kenny took a large wad of spitball and creamed it into my head. It pasted down my hair.

'There's no kicking!' shouted Mom.

'He's still doing it. They're both doing it.'

'You have to stop fighting. Put your brother on!'

I flung the phone onto the sofa, 'she wants to talk to you,' I said. 'You're in trouble, you're in trouble, you're in trouble,' I sang. My neck dripped in spit. It felt like a huge slimy cootie covering my entire head. Disgusting.

Mom shouted down the phone. 'Stop. Stop. Stop.' I knew she was sobbing at work. Could that get you fired?

I must have concentrated on Mom too much because a second later Kenny was close again.

He spit a shot into the center of my head. I dashed towards the kitchen. He followed close. I ducked down and rolled into a ball just when he was about to spit into the back of my head. He flew over me and smashed into the kitchen table. The chairs clanged and fell to the floor.

'What was that?!' I heard Mom shouting through the phone.

I ran back to the living room, but he caught me this time just as I grabbed the phone.

'I'll get you, UG!' he shouted

I was in an awkward position. I slipped on spit and David pried the phone from my hand. 'Mom? Mom?' he said into the receiver.

'You need to stop, David!'

'Ok, ok … I'm stopping. I'm stopping.' He handed the phone to Kenny. 'She wants to talk to you.'

He grabbed the phone and listened. I couldn't hear exactly what she said, but then he answered. 'Ok. We're going outside anyway.'

I could hear in his voice that it was over. I don't know how she changed his mind, but it ended suddenly like a flash. I scampered away towards the bathroom, closed the door and locked it even though they knew how to open it with a coat hanger.

I lay on the floor for a long time. My hair was matted in spitballs.

I lay there until the house became quiet … until I could hear the slap and ping of the basketball in the backyard. I could tell by the rhythm that the two of them were playing.

I eased myself up and looked in the bathroom mirror.

My face was ok … just a bit red, but drips of spit ran down my cheeks. I looked at myself for a long time. Spit on my face. Spitballs in my hair.

I looked into the mirror until I couldn't stand looking at myself anymore.

I sat on the toilet. The spitballs had clumped my hair together and it hung in chunks on the sides of my face.

I stared at the shower curtain across from me. It was meant to be blue and white with patterns of small fish swimming in a transparent sea. But it looked like the fish were swimming in an ocean of grayish black mold instead. Their stained dull eyes stared back at me. I don't know where the stain started but it seemed to grow up from the bottom of the curtain, out of the powder blue bathtub.

I studied the fish in the pattern. It was supposed to be a happy scene, to make you feel clean and bright in the shower, but it felt sad instead. Dirty. After a while, my cheeks began to itch.

I had to clean the spitballs out of my hair. I stood, leaned over the sink and started to pick them out. It was gross. I found a comb on the shelf and started combing. My hair was tangled in spit and paper. Tangled. Impossible. I didn't want any of it. I didn't want them on me. I didn't even want to be me.

I spied the scissors. They were the same ones mom used to cut the boys' hair. She would sit them on a kitchen chair in the tub beside the grey-eyed fish and give them a trim.

I picked up the scissors and lifted them to my own hair.

Do I dare? I thought.

I tried aiming at the spitballs at first. I snipped one and then another. But they clung to the strands of my hair like lice.

I turned the water on and rinsed my fingers. Disgusting.

I smelled the spit now, like boys' sticky bad breath.

I took hold of the scissors in my right hand and pulled out a length of hair with my left.

I think it was the smell mostly, but I felt like I had no choice.

I made the first cut. A wedge of sticky hair fell into the sink. I grabbed another.

Snip. And another. Snip.

I clipped the sides and bangs first.

Maybe that's enough. Maybe I can wash the rest out. I shouldn't just cut it all, should I? I wondered about what they would say at school. I wondered what Mom would say. But something in me just wanted it gone.

I reached for the back. It was impossible to see, though I turned and tried to look in the mirror.

My reflection revealed more spit and paper no matter which way I twisted my head, so I kept cutting.

I stopped when my hair was shorter than Kenny's but then I found some sticky spitball residue. So I cut some more and it was soon shorter than David's.

I could clearly see the white of my scalp.

I threw the disgusting clumps of spitball hair in the toilet and flushed. I waited until the tank filled and flushed again. Gone. I glanced at the grey fish on the curtains. For a moment they seemed to smile.

I turned the faucet on in the sink and washed my hands. I rubbed water through my hair.

It felt good shorter. It felt cleaner. But I couldn't wash the smell off with water. I needed something stronger. I lathered my head up with shampoo and was about to rinse when I saw mom's leg razor. It was pink with a purple circle in the middle. I remember the ad from TV … 'for the woman who wants every day to be easy.'

That's what mom wanted. Well I'd DO it. I'd make it easy. Or at least easier.

My hair was short now. And I was ready for a clean start.

I slid the razor over my head and it didn't feel like anything happened at all.

I ran it under the water and could see a small clump of hair wash away. I stroked the top of my head again and rinsed. Another small clump of hair. I kept stroking my head and rinsing until I could feel the difference when I ran my fingers on the top of my head.

Some spots were smooth where the scalp shone through, other areas were patchy and rough. There wasn't much lather left, so I rinsed my head and took a look. Tufts of hair stuck out unevenly, like brown grass popping up here and there.

I soaped up again.

I kept running the razor over my head and rinsing until I couldn't feel any hair on my head at all. I gave myself a final rinse and then I dried my scalp.

I was clean.

I was bald.

I looked just like a boy.

'I am UG,' I said.

Spilt Milk

The boys were still bouncing their basketball in the back yard when Mom came home.

I expected her to be mad and to try to ground me or something. I was nervous when I heard her park the car and turn off the engine. I balled myself up in the green armchair and pretended to read.

A cold chill swirled around my bald head. I rubbed my warm hands on my scalp, soothing.

I could hear Mom's steps as she approached the house between the slap and ping of the basketball bouncing in the backyard.

Slap, ping … click, as she opened the basement door.

Slap, ping … clonk, as she walked up the stairs.

Slap, ping … shuffle, as she moved through the kitchen.

Slap, ping … 'I'm home,' she said.

Slap ping … 'Hi, Mom,' I said in as casual a voice as I could muster.

Slap ping … Silence.

I could feel her standing in the doorway looking at me. She came into the living room and circled around the chair. I sunk deeper into the green cushion and shielded myself with my hard cover version of 'Calcio - The History of Italian Football.'

I'd borrowed it for my history project with Lorenzo.

But there wasn't much point in hiding. She would see me eventually. I had to face her.

I lowered the book.

When saw my head she didn't scream at me or turn red with anger. She just looked at me as if I were a curious creature or an animal that she'd never seen before.

She sat on the arm of the chair. I moved my arm to make room. The book slid down the side of the cushion. I could feel it. A shield if I needed one.

But she didn't poke at me. She was tender. She rubbed her fingers on my shiny scalp. She touched me like she used to when she came and read to me at night and stroked my hair as I fell asleep.

I had been ready for a fight. I had run through all kinds of excuses of why I did it. If she yelled, I would yell back. If she grounded me, I would just accept it.

I thought I was ready for everything, but I wasn't.

I wasn't ready to remember how she used to be when it felt like she loved me.

Her face quivered.

Her chin trembled.

A tear rolled down her cheek.

She kneeled in front of me and leaned forward.

The hard corner of 'Calcio' poked my thigh.

Mom pulled me in close and she hugged me.

I raised my arms and wrapped them around her back. I could feel her heavy breathing and her tears on the side of my bald head. They ran along my neck and down under my t-shirt.

She cupped the back of my head in the palm of her hands and rocked from side to side. I felt like I might cry too, but I didn't, because the moment that I thought I might, I noticed the slap-ping of the basketball had stopped. There were only a few seconds before my brothers would come back in.

I started to pull away from Mom's embrace a moment before the back door opened.

Mom looked into my eyes and then hugged me tightly again. When she let go, she rubbed her sleeve across her own eyes.

Kenny walked into the kitchen first. 'Mom?' he said.

She was kneeling in front of me now.

'Mom, are you ok? What's wrong?

The concern I heard in his voice made me think, for a moment, that he had his own story, that he could write the word 'kind' into it and it would stick like soccer was sticking to me.

But his concern turned into ridicule when he saw me, 'UG! Nice hairdo!'

And the glimmer of forgiveness that I felt flicked out like the light going out when a fuse pops in winter leaving the house in sudden, cold darkness.

Mom stood.

'Hey David, check out the UG,' said Kenny.

'Please, Kenny,' said Mom.

I balled my fists and covered my head with my forearms for a moment.

I heard David drop the basketball on the kitchen floor. It bounced on the linoleum tiles a few times before I looked up.

I lowered my arms. This was me.

'Whoa!' said David. 'Cool!'

I don't know what he meant by 'cool,'

Cool that I did it.

Cool because he was surprised.

Cool because I looked cool.

Or cool because I didn't look that different from him or any other boy at school.

Mom stood up. 'I'm going to make some supper. Rebecca, you can help me.'

'Mom, they call me UG.'

A confused glare washed over her face.

'Boys,' she said in a determined voice.

'You can call me UG too,' I said.

'I'm not calling you UG, Rebecca.'

She turned away from me. 'Boys, you can set the table.'

David had already disappeared into the bathroom.

'Kenny, take this,' she handed him the gallon jug of milk. He took it and placed it on the edge of the counter.

'I'll be right back,' he said.

At that moment, Mom turned from the fridge with a Tupperware bowl. The bottom of the bowl hit the milk jug with a perfect topspin because the jug flew off the counter and smashed onto the floor.

Milk exploded everywhere.

It drenched Mom. It splattered all the way up to my forehead. It covered the chairs and the table and created white patterns on the kitchen cupboards.

Mom look stunned. Everything moved in slow-motion like an instant replay.

Then she fell to her knees.

She wailed and tore at her wet blouse. She gripped her own hair and pulled.

Tears ran from her eyes. Snot ran from her nose.

I didn't know what else to do, so I side-stepped Mom, grabbed a dishtowel from the rack and started to soak up the milk.

'It's ok,' I said. 'I'll clean it up.'

I wrang the dishtowel out in the sink and turned the water on. The sound of running water merged with Mom's sobbing. I rinsed the towel and laid it flat over the largest puddle of milk. After it had absorbed the liquid, I picked it up and squeezed it in a ball over the sink again.

I kept going until the puddle was gone and then I started wiping down the chairs and the cupboard. It seemed impossible to sop up all the milk one towel at a time.

By the time I had finished, Mom's sobbing gave way to silent tears. I hung the towel over the faucet in the sink. Mom reached out for me.

I knelt in front of her.

She wrapped her arms around me.

I held her.

She cried.

Freestyling

One day you're invisible, the next everyone's talking about you.

Shave your head and see for yourself.

Girls who had never talked to me were suddenly asking all kinds of question. Whether they liked me or not is another thing. But other people were actually noticing me. It scared me a bit, but I liked it.

'Did your mom actually LET you cut off all of your hair?' asked Donna.

'I did it, didn't I?' I answered.

'But did you get permission?' asked Lisa.

'I don't need permission. I can do what I want.'

'Whatever you want?' asked Karen.

'Of course I can't do whatever I want, but when it comes to my body, or what clothes I wear or how I get my hair cut, it's up to me. I'm the boss.

'What about a tattoo?' said someone.

'They don't give kids tattoos!' I answered. 'But if they did, I could have one if I wanted.'

'My mom would never let me do something like that,' said Christine. 'Ever!'

I liked my new UG attitude. UG was a kicker. UG could do what she wanted when she wanted, but the Rebecca in me wanted to get away from these girls. Rebecca was telling me that as soon as the novelty ran off, they'd be just the way they always were … or worse.

Lorenzo saved me from them. Maybe he noticed me searching the group for some help, for a teammate. I was looking for a pass.

He pulled a ball out of his bag and kicked an easy high lob in my direction. I headed it up and then let it drop to my knee. I juggled it from knee to knee, down to my feet and kept it going. The group of girls took a step back and watched me go. I kept it up until a small group formed around me.

Foot, foot, foot, knee, knee. Foot, foot, up high. Head, head, head. Dramatic drop to foot and I caught it in the wedge between my shin and the top of my foot. I flicked it up and kicked a high lob over to Lorenzo who mirrored me move for move. He was good, better than me. He could copy almost anything I did and add in a few spins and turns.

He lobbed it over to me again and then we headed it back and forth to one another. Once, twice, three times. People started counting. 'Four, five, six, seven, eight, nine, ten, eleven…'

We kept juggling until Ms. Dunhill stepped into the center of the circle that had gathered around us. We were like performers in Quincy Market in Boston. All we needed was a boom box and some pumping music.

Ms. Dunhill glared at the crowd and then at us. 'Stop this at once!' she said.

I lost my concentration and looked up at her.

The ball shot wildly from my knee and would have hit her square in the belly if Lorenzo hadn't saved it. He reached out, pulled the ball back and stuffed it into his bag.

'You two!' Ms. Dunhill's cheeks turned bright red. 'Follow me,' she said.

We followed her to her office and were told to sit in two chairs and wait just outside the door in the faculty wing.

Lorenzo said, 'Should we work on our football project after school?'

'Yeah. Sure,' I said. 'Let's meet in the library at two-thirty … If we don't get expelled.'

Mr. McCartney rounded the corner and walked towards us. 'Heard you two put on a pretty good show.'

'Good enough to get us in trouble,' I said.

Mr. McCartney glanced down. Lorenzo's ball had emerged from the top of his bag as round and smooth as my bald head.

'This the culprit?' Mr. McCartney picked up the ball.

He studied it close to his nose. He squeezed it slightly.

'It seems like it's behaving exactly as a ball should behave,' he said.

He gave it a sniff, which I thought was a little gross. But it also looked kind of funny.

'Smells like an ordinary soccer ball.'

He dropped it suddenly from nose level.

I felt my eyes open wide.

The ball didn't bounce on the floor. Mr. McCartney tapped it up with his foot and it landed back in his hands by his nose as if it were a yo-yo on a string.

'Let's try that again,' he said. He dropped it and tapped it up again. The only sound it made was a mini thud when it hit the top of this shoe.

He didn't even move his hands. The ball landed between them with precision.

He handed the ball back to Lorenzo.

'Better keep an eye on that thing,' he said.

The door opened to Ms. Dunhill's room. The small metal sign on her door said Vice Principal but it could have said 'Dean of Discipline.'

'Lorenzo,' she said. 'Rebecca.'

I was about to correct her but she turned and we followed her into the room.

'I would like to start by saying that I admire your skill. I know that you must practice a lot to be able to bounce the ball like that.'

She paused.

I smiled. We're not going to get in trouble, I thought.

'However … Ball sports are not allowed in the school or break out areas except for in the gym or on the playing field. This is a hard, fast rule and it must be obeyed.'

She stared Lorenzo down until he bowed his head and looked down into his lap. Then she looked at me. Our eyes locked and I held her gaze. I wasn't trying to win a staring contest with her, but it turned into one.

The trick is to keep your eyes open and to look like you're aiming to see right through to the back of your opponent's head. Just like when you're kicking a ball. You aim for a meter behind the ball and that'll make it shoot in exactly the direction you choose.

'Understood,' said Ms. Dunhill. She kept her gaze on me.

'Understood,' I repeated.

She turned to Lorenzo. 'Understood, Lorenzo.'

'Yes, Ms. Dunhill.'

'Now, Lorenzo, you may be excused. I'd like to speak for a few minutes with Rebecca.'

That name again.

'Ok, Ms. Dunhill,' said Lorenzo. He stood, grabbed his bag and left the room.

He glanced back just as he was leaving the room and passed me a quick smile. It sent a warm feeling through me.

Ms. Dunhill smiled at me too now, but her smile made me feel uncertain and small.

'Rebecca,' she said. 'When a student does something as drastic as cutting off all of their hair, there's usually something behind it. I'd like to ask you why you decided to shave your hair off. Is that ok?'

'Yes,' I said. I figured I'd just tell the truth. 'My hair was tangled and I started to cut it and then I just kept going and going.'

'It must have been very tangled,' she said.

'It was,' I said.

'Did you have gum in it? Because I remember once getting gum in my hair and I didn't want to cut my hair but there was no other way. I cried for two weeks. But you don't seem sad about it.'

'No, I'm not sad. I'm glad that I did it.'

'Was it gum that was tangled in your hair?'

'No,' I said.

'A normal tangle wouldn't lead you to cut your hair so drastically, don't you think?'

'Probably not?'

'Well, what was caught in your hair?'

'Spitballs,' I said.

'Spitballs?'

She looked confused.

'Spitballs are tiny balls of paper that you chew on and then spit through a straw at someone. They're very …'

She interrupted. 'Yes,' she said, 'I know what spitballs are. But spitballs are small. You can just give them a rinse and they'll disappear.'

'Not these spitballs,' I said.

I didn't feel sad exactly. More humiliated, And frustrated. Afraid. And I didn't want to talk about HOW I cut my hair. Tears swelled in my eyes. I rubbed them and it was like popping water balloons.

I wiped my cheeks, trying to dry up the tears. I didn't want to cry. I didn't want to cry. But my sleeves weren't big enough to sop up the flow.

I wanted to be UG. Bald UG.

But I was Rebecca and I couldn't keep her inside any longer and hide behind UG.

Rebecca rushed up and out of me and there was no way I could stop the flood.

After School

The worst trouble you can get into isn't when they yell at you, it's when they pretend to be nice to you or concerned about you. Then you're in big, big trouble.

It wasn't only me that got into trouble for cutting my hair and shaving my head.

My brothers both got into heaps of trouble too. My mom yelled at them and told them if they ever did anything like that to me again, they would be grounded for the rest of the year.

But even they didn't get into the most trouble.

It was Mom who got into the most trouble.

I didn't know that cutting my hair off would cause such a big problem for her, but it did. I don't know if the woman that sat in our living room was from the schools or from Social Services but she seemed official. Her deep blue skirt, her light blue blouse and her black high heeled shoes all looked official.

Even though Mom never hit me or was mean to me herself, she was in trouble because of what she let my brothers do. I told the woman that she didn't 'let' them do it. They did it themselves when Mom wasn't around.

Mom had to work. I knew that. Work was important.

If she didn't work, we wouldn't even have food or a house or anything. That would be a bigger problem than me chopping off my hair because of spitballs. Having no money would be a big problem for all of us.

The woman said that nine-year-olds should not be left home alone.

Mom cried and cried and cried.

'But she wasn't alone,' said Mom to the woman. 'Her brothers were looking after her.'

'May I be dismissed?' I used my most polite voice.

'No,' said the woman. 'I think it's important for you to be here right now.'

I sidled up to my Mom and put my hand on her thigh, something I usually never did.

Mom rubbed my back.

The woman nodded and I cuddled closer to Mom.

I didn't want Mom to be in trouble. If I'd known she would get into such trouble, I would have washed my hair. It might have taken a while, but I could have done it. I didn't cut my hair to get Mom into trouble.

The woman said, 'You need a better solution. Your two boys are not qualified to take care of a ten-year-old.'

My mind raced through possible solutions, but the best one, the first one that I thought of was that I could go to Lorenzo's. 'Lorenzo's mom could take me.'

'No, Rebecca,' said Mom.

'Who's Lorenzo?' asked the woman.

'He's my best friend and his mom is always home.'

Mom stopped crying for a moment. 'She has a toddler. I'm sure she's got her hands full. She wouldn't want to have someone else there every afternoon.'

'She would, she would, she would. She loves me!' I said.

That made Mom burst into tears again, sobbing louder than before.

I didn't mean that Mom didn't love me too, as much … more. I just meant that Lorenzo's mom wouldn't mind. I knew that she wouldn't mind.

It felt as if I kicked the ball into my own goal by accident. The woman looked like a referee who could hardly believe it herself. She held off on blowing the whistle.

'I'm never a problem when I'm there. I help take care of Marco. He's adorable.'

'Marco?' said the woman.

Mom wiped away her tears, 'The baby. Rebecca likes to help out.'

'I bet you're good with him,' said the woman.

'Oh, yes!' I said. 'I get to feed him. He's so funny when he eats. And when he poos, you can see it by the way he squeezes up his eyes.' I made a face like Marco and the woman chuckled. It made Mom smile too and she patted my back again.

'Ok,' said Mom. 'I'll talk to her.'

'Yes,' said the woman. 'And I need to talk to her too.'

Mom started to say something but the woman stared her down. That woman could have stared me down if she wanted to. I had finally met someone who could beat me in a staring contest. I wondered if the woman had older brothers who used to beat on her too.

When Mom left the room to call Lorenzo's mom I sank into the green armchair. I didn't want to wait there with the woman, but I had no choice. I couldn't just leave her there alone in the living room. I could feel her watching me. I scanned the room to look at anything but her stare. I didn't dare look her in the eyes.

I spotted my book about Italian soccer and picked it up.

I made the mistake of looking up at the woman as I sat back on the chair.

'You like soccer?' she said.

'Yeah,' I nodded. 'I'm writing a report on it for History class. The history of soccer. In Italian they call it *calcio*.'

'Yes,' said the woman. 'My Dad is a great fan of Italian soccer. He loves Lazio.'

'Me too!' I said. 'And Lorenzo too. His dad is our soccer coach,' I said.

Mom came back at the exact second I said it. 'Your soccer coach?' she said.

I didn't answer.

The woman looked at me and then at mom and then at me again.

I saw a flash of anger on Mom's face. I knew the woman saw it too.

'Well, how did it go?' asked the woman, 'is she willing to meet with me?'

'Yes,' said Mom.

The woman's calming smile relaxed me. She sat back down. 'So, Rebecca,' she said. 'Tell me about your soccer.'

'I, uh …'

I didn't know whether to tell the whole story or not.

'Start from the beginning,' said the woman.

'Well, I used to be on the girl's soccer team, but Mom made me quit,' I said.

The woman's eyes blasted lasers at Mom.

'It was impossible to do practice as well as everything else that needs to be done on Saturdays. Especially when you have to work all week. I need time to get the house in order, do laundry, that sort of thing.'

'That's not why!' I jumped in. 'It's because it doesn't work with my brothers' baseball schedule. You said that it's more important to take them instead of me.'

'That's not true,' said Mom.

'It is,' I said.

The woman sat up in her chair.

Now, I was getting Mom in trouble on purpose. But I didn't care because she was lying. Or maybe it was the UG in me that didn't care because I saw Mom searching for an answer to give to the woman.

So I kept talking, 'But I'm glad I don't play on that girls' team anymore. I'm playing on Lorenzo's team. I was invited by his dad. He's the coach. It's a boys team. All boys. And I'm one of them. I'm just as good as they are too. Better than a lot of them.'

It felt good to tell Mom. And it felt safe to do it with the woman there. It's easier to talk when you don't think you'll get into a fight.

'You look like a soccer player,' said the woman. 'What position do you play?'

'I'm a midfielder. A left wing. Lorenzo's dad says I can be great.'

'That's nice, Rebecca' said the woman.

Mom didn't say a word.

'There's another thing,' I said. Talking about soccer made me feel strong. 'I have a nickname too. They call me UG,' I said.

'UG?' asked the woman.

'Rebecca, stop, please,' said Mom. 'You need to stop this and go upstairs until you can stop lying.'

'I'm not lying,' I said. 'It's you who's lying. You said I couldn't play soccer because of Kenny and David's baseball and you never clean the house or do the laundry. That's a lie too!'

'Rebecca,' said Mom.

'UG,' I said. I was standing now, in front of the green chair.

The woman spoke one tone louder. 'I'd like both of you to stop.'

That shut us up.

I collapsed back into the chair and Mom's head dropped into her hands.

The woman leaned in my direction. 'UG?' she said, 'where does the nick name come from?'

'My brothers call me that. I used to hate it, but now I love it,' I said.

'You love it?' asked the woman.

'Yes,' I said. 'I am UG.'

'Well, then, UG,' said the woman, 'It's nice to meet you.'

She stretched out her hand.

I took it.

When I first looked at her, I thought everything about that woman would be official, hard cut and dry, but her hand was soft and warm. I looked into her eyes again, and those eyes told me that it was ok to call myself whatever I wanted.

Her gaze was steady. Firm. Her eyes were like the sweet spot on a soccer ball. If you met them in exactly the right way, they knocked you to the stratosphere.

She smiled at me.

'Our time is up for today,' she said. 'I'll contact you with a new time and I'll also make contact with your neighbor if you give me her details. It would be best if we could sort out some other arrangement as soon as possible.'

'I could just go there after school tomorrow,' I said. 'Lorenzo and I have to work on our report anyway.'

'Okay with you?' the woman looked at Mom.

Mom nodded, 'Yes. That's ok.'

On the Couch

Mom collapsed onto the couch after the woman left.

We had to make our own supper.

Kenny was good at frying frozen hamburgers, so we ate them with some oven fries. I set the table and David came in when everything was ready. I made a plate for Mom. I melted a slice of provolone cheese on top and even put a dollop of Gulden's mustard on the side, the way she liked it, but she didn't move from the couch.

After supper, my brothers watched TV. I sat on the green armchair and read 'Calcio.' I looked up every now and then when I heard a good car chase or a love scene. That's what I like, car chases and love scenes. My brothers like car chases and fights.

I hated fights, so I never watch much TV, at least not when my brothers are around. They tell the boys at school not to hit but then every show on TV has one person hitting another, even the nice shows like 'Little House on the Prairie' have fistfights in them. I like shows like

'American Idol' and 'America's Got Talent' because they're about real people doing cool things.

I also like Mr. Bean who is an old-fashioned English guy who plays mean but funny tricks on people. He does things like pressing all the buttons on the elevator when it's full of people so they have to stop at every floor. He's silly. And you can learn lots of good annoying things from him that you can try out yourself.

Movies are like TV shows, but worse. Everyone's fighting. But I don't care so much when it comes to movies. I love to go to the movies. I love sitting in the seat, leaning back and munching on popcorn. I love the trailers for other films too. They always give you a sneak peek about what's coming soon.

Mr. McCartney says if an alien race were ever to land on earth in the future and watched all of the films and TV shows that we've made they'd think that all we ever did was fight. That's what we'd leave behind.

Car chases are cool because you never really see anyone get hurt. I know that they're not real because if you did some of the things that they do on TV you would get hurt or even die.

Last summer, on the street in front of our house, Mr. Bennet's dog, Bella, was run over. We were all outside on our way to Arcadia State Park when we heard the crunch and squeal of tires. The driver was a woman from out of town who started crying as soon as she got out of the car. Mr. Bennet ran out onto the front steps and into the road. He started crying too. Everyone started crying, except Kenny who grabbed a beach towel and scooped Bella up.

He put pressure on the huge gash on Bella's leg like he'd been taught in his Boy Scout first-aid class. He told mom to rush to the vet's. So we all hopped in the car.

Kenny sat in the front with Bella. Mr. Bennet sat in the back seat with me and David. Mr. Bennet was shaky, so I held his hand.

When we got to the vet's Kenny was the first one out the door and inside.

Bella lost her leg, but the vet told us that Kenny had saved Bella's life.

I don't know how she did it, but Bella could still run pretty good with only three legs. She chased squirrels and birds, but she never ran in the road again.

I thought about how impossible it would be to play soccer with only one leg. But people do amazing things. I saw a program once about a guy who was born with no legs and only small stumps for arms but he could swim and play tennis and lots of other things.

Mom hadn't moved all night. I don't even think she blinked.

I closed my book and leaned forward to be able to see the clock in the kitchen.

We're supposed to be in bed by 9. Mom usually says, 'It's time to brush your teeth,' at around 8.30 and the boys do it at the next commercial break.

It was 8.52 I scissor kicked myself up and out of the chair. 'Well…I'm off to brush my teeth and then to bed,' I said.

Everyone ignored me.

You'd think being ignored would be better than being picked on, but it's not.

When you're ignored, it's like you don't exist. And if you don't exist, then you don't matter to anyone.

I shuffled to the bathroom, balanced 'Calcio' on the edge of the sink and started to brush. I usually don't look at myself when I brush my teeth. I usually sit on the edge of the tub or on the toilet and brush away until I'm ready to spit.

But today I looked.

I rubbed my fingers along the top of my scalp as I brushed. I could feel that my hair was already starting to grow out. That was fast. I decided that if it grew more I'd shave it again.

A lot of soccer players have shaved heads but some of them have really long hair too. Some have tattoos. I imagined what I'd look like with a tattoo on my arm. Maybe a panther. But not a pink one. Dark purple, with paw prints leading down my arm.

I brushed my teeth some more and rinsed my mouth, careful not to get 'Calcio' wet.

I walked back through the living room.

'Goodnight,' I said.

'Night UG,' said David.

Kenny ignored me.

Mom didn't say anything either.

I had a stack of soccer magazines on the side of my bed. I leafed through them, looking at the pictures, imagining myself on the field, playing against the best in the world. Maybe I'd play for the US in the Olympics one day.

A steady stream of sound came from the TV downstairs.

I don't know what time the boys actually went to bed, but Mom was still on the couch when I got up in the morning. It didn't seem like she had moved at all.

'Good morning, Mom,' I said.

She didn't answer.

I sat down next to her and she didn't move aside, but I squeezed myself onto the sofa anyway. I stroked her hair. She was awake, but didn't look at me, though she did blink a few times.

The rest of the house was quiet. The boys probably wouldn't get up unless someone told them too.

I left the couch and called upstairs, 'Kenny, David! It's time for breakfast. We have to get ready for school.'

I stood in front of Mom. 'Mom, Mom,' I said. 'We have to get ready for school and you have to get ready for work.'

She didn't answer.

'Mom, you're scaring me. Why aren't you answering me?'

She blinked, so I knew she was alive, but she didn't say anything.

'Are you sick?' I asked.

She didn't answer.

'Well, I have to get ready or I'll be late.'

The boys came down after a while. They walked right past Mom and made their breakfast. I was already tucking into my frozen blueberries and muesli.

'Doesn't Mom have to get ready for work too?' I said to Kenny and David.

Kenny glanced over to Mom on the couch. 'Yeah, of course,' he said.

The three of us put our dishes in the dishwasher and went to the couch. 'Mom,' said Kenny. 'It's time to get ready for work.'

'Mom,' said David. 'Are you ok?'

'You have to answer us,' I said.

David knelt in front of her. He stroked her eyebrows. I squeezed myself back onto the couch next to her.

Kenny spoke louder, 'Mom, Mom. You have to work.'

She blinked and then it looked like she was waking from a dream. 'Get me the phone, will you David?'

'Are you ok, Mom?' I asked.

'I have a headache, but I'll be ok. You can all go on to school. I've got to call in sick.'

I wondered if that meant that I couldn't go to Lorenzo's as I had planned.

David handed her the phone.

'You all should go,' she said. 'You'll be late.'

The three of us backed away from the couch and headed downstairs to fetch our jackets. None of us spoke about Mom while we were waiting. I don't know what the boys thought. I don't even know what I thought.

Sometimes you're just sick. I've felt like that before. So sick that I didn't want to move.

The bus came.

We hopped on.

Kenny and David disappeared to the back. I sat up front. I pulled my hoodie up over my head. Kids stared at my bald head otherwise. Today I didn't want anyone to notice me.

I went to school and then I went to Lorenzo's. We practiced in his yard and then we did our homework at his kitchen table while his Mom made supper. Lorenzo and I fed Marco. I was in charge of the spoon and he took the sippy cup.

We ate when Lorenzo's dad came home.

When it was time for me to go home Lorenzo and his dad walked with me until we came to the backyard of our house. They waited on the empty lot across the street until I walked into the gate and up the back steps to the house.

I waved. They waved back.

I walked inside.

The TV was on. Kenny and David were watching another car chase. Mom was still on the couch.

My Fault

It was my fault.

I thought about Mom a couple of times during the day while I was at school. But I figured she'd be ok when I got home from Lorenzo's.

She didn't say 'Hi' when I came in or 'goodnight,' when I went to bed. Two nights in a row. I've been sick before, but I've always managed to at least say 'goodnight,' to her and to my brothers, even though they didn't always answer.

Mom slept on the couch. I wondered if she had moved at all during the day. She had to have gotten up to go to the bathroom. But she must have done it during the day, when no one was looking because there was no sign that she had peed on the couch or anything and no one can hold it that long.

I smuggled a soccer ball up to my room and I lay on my back with my legs in the air. I balanced the ball on the souls of my feet, popping it up now and then and catching it with my toes.

I leafed through a book with pictures of the best soccer players of all time. Lorenzo and I could write a whole paper just about Pelé. He played a long time ago for Brazil. He has a smile on his face in every picture I've seen of him, even the action shots. Lorenzo's dad agrees that Pelé was best, even though he's not Italian.

I tapped the ball from one foot to the other, back and forth, faster and faster, higher and higher. I heard the TV turn off. I glanced at the clock. 9.30 pm.

The house fell silent for a moment and then I heard water running in the pipes. They must be brushing their teeth. The water turned off. I lay still, balancing the soccer ball, listening with the book open on my belly.

'Night, Mom,' said David. His voice sounded muffled as it traveled up the stairs and through my closed door.

'Goodnight, Mom,' said Kenny.

I didn't hear her answer, although I wouldn't have, if she were answering quietly.

They came upstairs. The door to their room opened and closed. The house fell quiet again. I listened for a long time.

I folded my book and let the ball drop onto the bed beside me. I switched off my reading light and rested my head in my hands. I stroked the ends of my growing hair. Rubbing the soft and bristly hair under my fingers made my scalp tingle. It felt like petting a kitten.

I rubbed and rubbed in circles.

My mind spun in circles too. And then it struck me.

Mom was sick because of me. She was sick because I shaved my head. She was sick because the woman from Social Services had come over.

I stopped stroking my head as the first tear fell. It ran down the side of my cheek into my ear. Soon it was raining tears.

'It's my fault,' I cried softly. 'It's my fault.'

I wanted to cry out, but I didn't want the boys to hear. I tried to shake it off, like when someone kicks you in the shin and it hurts so much that you want to die. That's how it felt, only inside my belly.

Mom had collapsed on the couch because of me.

She couldn't work because of me.

We would run out of money because of me.

We would be forced to move because of me.

We would all die because of me.

I cried for a long time, alone, until my tears ran out. Until I knew that the boys would be asleep.

I slipped out of bed and crept downstairs.

The curtains were open in the living room and the room was lit by the streetlights and the moon. Mom lay still. I walked up to her and bent down close so that I could see her face.

She was drooling like she did on Saturday mornings.

I stroked her hair. It was long and soft but only half of her head was showing so I couldn't really rub her scalp the way that I had done my own.

I leaned against the side of the couch and rested my head on the bit of the cushion that was showing between her chin and her chest. Just enough for my bald head.

I became so thirsty that I had to get up and get a drink. I left Mom and went into the kitchen, but I didn't turn the lights on. I got a drink of water, then I thought that Mom must be thirsty too. So I re-filled the glass and brought it back to the living room.

'Mom, mom,' I whispered. 'I've brought you some water.'

Her mouth moved but the rest of her was completely still. I lifted the glass to her lips but there was no way to get her to drink with her lying on her side.

I placed the glass on the coffee table and went back to the kitchen to find a straw. They were always in the third drawer from the top on the right hand side of the stove. I found one and padded back into the living room.

I inserted the straw and lifted it to Mom's lips. Fortunately, it was one of those straws that you could bend on the top. I call them worm straws because the bendy bit makes them look a bit like worms.

I bent it to her lips and saw with relief that her mouth formed a circle around the end of the straw. I let her drink. She didn't even open her eyes, but soon I heard the slurp at the bottom of the empty glass.

I went to the kitchen and re-filled it.

Mom drank up most of that one too.

I placed the glass on the coffee table.

There wasn't much room on the couch, but I lifted the quilt and squeezed myself in down low behind Mom's legs. I wrapped my arms up and around her waist with my head on her hip.

When she slept, Mom didn't get warm like I did. Her body was cool and her toes were cold against my shins. I lifted one leg and allowed her feet to poke through behind my calf muscles so they would warm up.

This was my fault and I had to do something about it.

I would do anything.

Anything.

Mad Dash

The next morning was a mad dash.

I don't know what time I fell asleep, but when I woke up, lying next to Mom, I had five minutes to make the bus. There was no way to wake the boys, get dressed, eat breakfast, brush my teeth and make it to school on time.

'Mom, we're late!' I shout-whispered as I hopped off the couch.

His eyes popped open.

Perhaps it was the urgency in my voice or maybe Mom just felt a bit better, but she sat up on the couch. I called from the bottom of the stairs, 'Kenny! David! Come. We're late for school.'

I turned back towards the couch after calling them. Mom looked tired, but she was sitting. She rubbed her eyes and held out her arms. I ran to her, kneeled in front of her and hugged her.

I felt her hand on my back and then it slid up to touch the back of my head. She stroked my short hair. She held me tight and then pulled back and kissed my forehead.

The boys trundled down the stairs.

'Why didn't you wake us?' said Kenny.

'Yeah,' said David. 'We'll never make it in time.'

Mom's arms dropped.

I stood up.

'It's not my job to wake you up for school,' I said.

'Why do you always do it then?' said Kenny.

'Because you never get up on your own,' I said.

'If you always do it, then it's your job. Isn't it UG?' said Kenny.

He said UG in such an ugly and nasty way that I quivered inside.

'Yeah … UG!' agreed David.

Right then, I wished that I were pinned onto the green chair so that I could kick them both wildly. Maybe I'd land a chin shot.

'Please,' whispered Mom.

We turned. It was the first word that she'd muttered in days.

'No fighting. I can't take any more fighting,' she said softly.

I left the bottom of the stairs and went straight for my blueberries and muesli.

I popped the first one into my mouth and sucked on it. As the coldness faded into blueberry flavor, I added milk and it froze, coating the blueberries in a milky white film.

I sat at the table, eating as quickly as I could.

Mom lifted herself off the couch and made her way to the bathroom.

My brothers rushed around in the kitchen, making their own breakfast.

Kenny turned to me, 'We'll get you later, UG.' He said.

I stuck out my tongue.

I was happy that I didn't have to come straight home after school. Now I could go to Lorenzo's, and we could play soccer, and I could feed Marco.

Kenny tried to stare me down but I stared back. He slid his finger along the base of his neck motioning that he was going to cut my head off. 'Dead,' he mouthed.

I ate as quickly as I could. Mom was in the bathroom, turning the water on and off. I imagined her fixing her hair, brushing her teeth, rubbing on make-up, putting her face on.

If we were late for school, she was late for work too, if she was planning on going today.

The boys were quiet when they ate. They wolfed their food down like dogs. I downed all my cereal, popped the last blueberry in my mouth and lifted the bowl to my lips.

Blueberry flavored milk. It was probably the best part of breakfast. I drank it down and left the table before the boys had finished.

I was rinsing my bowl when Mom re-entered the kitchen. She was wearing a blue skirt and a blouse. She had her nylons on and was jabbing an earring in as she walked towards us.

'We'll miss the bus,' I said.

'I'll have to take you,' she said. 'You boys finish up.'

I had rushed to get ready and now I'd have to wait for a ride. 'I'll see if I can catch it anyway,' I said.

'I've got to take the boys anyway,' she said.

I wanted to run out there and then. I could have made it, but I didn't want Mom to feel bad again, so I said, 'Ok.'

I grabbed my backpack. 'I'll wait downstairs.'

I took my time to walk down the stairs, grab my jacket and open the door. The bus passed as I walked out. If I had run before, I would have made it.

I sat on the wall in front of the house. Waiting.

Kenny and David burst out of the door.

'I'm sitting in the front,' said Kenny. He pushed David aside.

'No! It's my turn. You sat in front last time,' shouted David tackling Kenny like a pro back fielder.

I stood up, looped my backpack over my shoulder and walked towards the car.

'I think it's Rebecca's turn,' said Mom.

'NO WAY!' shouted both of them.

'I don't mind,' I said. I just wanted to get to school. I hated being late.

'I said it's Rebecca's turn,' repeated Mom.

Kenny took advantage of the distraction, pushed David to the side, ran around the front of the car opened the door and hopped into the front seat.

David gave him the finger, but made sure Mom couldn't see.

I flung my backpack onto the back seat and climbed in. It was better to have David beside me than Kenny. Kenny would always give me a kick. David just ignored me.

Mom sat in the driver's seat and started the engine. She shifted the car into reverse and reached back with her right arm. She lifted it over the passenger seat turning to see the driveway behind us.

The morning light bounced off the hood of the car and shone through her soft fine brown hair revealing her scalp under it.

I wondered how she would look with her head shaved.

She concentrated on backing the car out.

Her make-up, eyeliner and mascara couldn't hide the black and blue puffs under her eyes. She seemed older and bruised, as if she had been struck on the bridge of her nose by a soccer ball.

The Less You Say

Lorenzo and I walked from the bus stop toward his house. Even though we lived close to one another, he was on a different route. That meant that I didn't have to ride in the same bus as my brothers.

A car was pulling out of Lorenzo's driveway. I recognized it at once, and hopped behind a lilac bush, dragging Lorenzo with me. It was the woman from Social Services.

Lorenzo's mom stood by the car and chatted to the woman. She held Marco in her arms and bounced him as she spoke.

I don't know why I didn't want to see her. She was nice to me. She gave me permission to be at Lorenzo's.

It's one thing when you choose to have a friend come over and a completely different thing when your friend 'has' to come over because some Social Worker says so.

Lorenzo knelt beside me. 'What?' he said.

He hadn't seen the car yet or at least he hadn't noticed it. I crouched down lower.

'Let's pretend that we're spies and that we have to sneak into the house without being seen,' I said. 'We can run around back, climb in through your window and pretend that we'd been in your room for hours. Your mom will be shocked.'

'Sounds cool,' said Lorenzo.

'Ok,' I said, flattening out a bit of dirt. I snapped off a dried out lilac twig and started drawing. 'This is your house. You can flank around to the right and I'll take the left.'

I drew semi-circles around the house. 'We'll meet in the back, climb up the bulkhead and slip into the window. Then we can surprise your mom.'

'Maybe we can sneak into the kitchen and snatch some cookies before she sees us,' he said.

'That sounds like a good idea,' I said. 'Any questions?'

I kept one eye on the house, the car had pulled away.

'No, it sounds like a cool plan,' said Lorenzo.

'Alright,' I said. 'The coast is clear. Make sure you keep your head down.'

He nodded.

'Ok, in three, two, one …' I crouched down and dashed across the open lot. Lorenzo ran to the right. Once we reached the side of the house, we both booked it as fast as we could and were soon standing on the bulkhead.

Lorenzo tried to push up the window, but it was locked. I was on my tiptoes, helping him push, when I slid down the metal bulkhead. It gonged when I hit the bottom.

Lorenzo's mom poked her head out the kitchen window.

'Mission abort … mission abort,' said Lorenzo. 'We've been spotted.'

'You're home,' said his Mom. 'What are you two up to?'

'We're spies,' I said.

'Ok, spy kids. Why not come in and have a snack?'

Lorenzo bent his knees and slid down the bulkhead too. He was off as soon as his feet touched the grass, and the race was on.

He was quicker than me in short distances, but I could run fast for longer. He had the lead until we took the corner around to the front of the house and then I caught up. We were neck in neck as we hit the front door.

'Shhhh,' said Lorenzo's mom as we swung the door open.

'Tie,' I said.

'Tie,' said Lorenzo at exactly the same time.

'Marco's having a nap,' said Lorenzo's mom as we walked through the door.

Lorenzo and I hushed immediately. I walked over and took a long look at Marco.

Lorenzo's mom handed Lorenzo a plastic tray. 'Why not take this outside and play for a while until Marco gets up?'

'Ok, Mamma,' said Lorenzo, taking the tray. There were two sandwiches and slices of apples, plus two bananas.

'Here, Rebecca,' you can take this. She handed me a plastic Tupperware jug of apple juice and two matching cups.

'Thanks, I said.'

She smiled at me and I felt guilty.

I wondered what that social services woman had said to Lorenzo's Mom.

Something in the way she looked at me felt different. I had thought it would be so easy and so perfect to just come here after school. What was there to talk about? But now Lorenzo's mom knew. And that would mean that his dad would know too. Maybe he already did.

I wondered if they had talked about it. I wonder if they had to decide if it was ok for me to come over now … every day, after school.

I had always felt welcomed here and now I felt like I was breaking in.

I stood with the jug. Still. Quiet. It was only a moment's pause but when I looked up into Lorenzo's mom's eyes she gave me one of those 'poor you' looks. Just a little one, but it was there.

'Are you coming?' Lorenzo held the door open with his foot.

'Yeah. I'm coming.'

I followed him out.

We sat at the table on the side of the house and ate our snack. I was quiet.

'You okay?' asked Lorenzo.

'Yeah. I'm good,' I said. But I didn't feel good. I had an urge to run home and fight with my brothers. I would have loved to give Kenny a good kick in the shins.

Lorenzo had finished his sandwich and was tugging on an apple slice.

'Let's practice,' he said.

I stood with my sandwich still in my hands. A soccer ball was lodged in the shrubs on the side of the house. Lorenzo kicked it free, out into the yard.

I ate as we passed the ball back and forth, warming up.

'Should we do some drills?' I asked.

'Sure,' said Lorenzo.

He loved drills and I usually just wanted to play free. Lorenzo's dad said that the best players do drills, and they see drills as part of play.

He said if you have fun in the drills then your free play will shine.

Lorenzo grabbed some plastic cones and laid them out in a line on the grass. 'Let's do three passes and shoot,' he said.

He ran down one side of the cones and I ran down the other. We passed through the cones three times and then the last person shot. It was hard to keep pace, pass perfectly and make a high-quality shot at the end. You can't look at the other person the whole time. You have to feel them and anticipate that they are in position and pass between the cones.

Timing and trust make it work.

Lorenzo was great at speeding up or slowing down to make the most of my average passing. Those times when we hit the rhythm perfectly were great. It felt like we were unstoppable. But for every perfect run we had about five that didn't work.

It felt great to be working, concentrating on footwork and improving. Practicing made me forget Mom and my brothers.

We did about thirty-five passes and started getting it right more and more often.

'Should we take a break?' I said, trying to catch my breath.

Lorenzo said, 'Why don't we go for ten perfect runs in a row then we'll stop.' He sounded just like his dad.

Lorenzo will be a great player and a great coach someday too.

It took us two more hours but we finally managed to make ten perfect runs in a row.

Lorenzo's dad rolled in from work and waved to us.

I'd forgotten all about the woman visiting from Social Services. I'd forgotten that I 'had' to be there. Everything was perfect until Lorenzo's mom called us in for supper and we sat at the table.

At home, we never talked about anything.

But at Lorenzo's they talked about everything.

And that day 'everything' might be me.

Weird

Lorenzo's mom ladled a sweet pepper tomato sauce over a large dish of steaming pasta. She grated cheese on top. It smelled amazing.

A bowl of cauliflower that she had sautéed with raisins and garlic was already on the table. Whenever I ate cauliflower in the past it had been boiled and I hated it. But this was different. It smelled delicious.

Lorenzo's dad helped to serve. I was starved.

'Everyone,' Lorenzo's mom called attention with a formality in her voice that made us all sit up. 'I'd like this to be a family meeting dinner.'

I'd never been to a family meeting before and the worried look on Lorenzo's face told me that there could be something to worry about.

I knew what was coming.

'I didn't do it,' said Lorenzo's dad with a glum look on his face that mirrored Lorenzo's. 'It must have been the cat,' he said with a smile.

'Dad, we don't have a cat,' said Lorenzo.

'Then who did it?' teased Lorenzo's dad.

'I dunno,' said Lorenzo.

'Well, if it wasn't me and it wasn't the cat, then who?'

Lorenzo looked at me. I looked at him. He looked back at his dad who started to laugh.

'Ok,' said Lorenzo's mom. 'Enough silliness. No one did anything. And if they did, I'm sure it was you, Emilio.' She reached across the table and pinched Lorenzo's dad's cheek.

'I have something that I'd like to say,' she paused.

I knew she was going to say something about me and for a split second, I thought about running off.

'From now on after school Rebecca will come here,' she said.

'Every day?' asked Lorenzo.

Why did he ask that? Did he not want time to come every day?

'Yes. Every day,' continued his mom. 'You'll wait for each other, ride the bus together and come here. Ok?'

'Yeah,' said Lorenzo. 'We can practice.'

'You can do your homework first and then you can practice.'

'Is that ok with you, Rebecca?'

'Yes, please,' I said.

Lorenzo's mom continued. 'That means that I expect you to come here. Do you know what I mean, Rebecca?'

'Yeah, that I come here instead of going home.'

'Yes, instead of going home … or … anywhere else.'

I didn't really understand. Where else would I go anyway? But I nodded.

Lorenzo's dad reached out and took Lorenzo's hand. 'This means that you wait for each other. You look after each other, like on the field. You understand?'

'Yes, I understand,' said Lorenzo.

'You understand?' He looked at me.

'Yes,' I said. 'We look after each other,' I said.

'Is there anything else that anyone would like to bring up?' asked Lorenzo's mom.

Marco grunted at that second and we all turned to look at him. His face scrunched up tight. He let out a huge fart sound and I knew that he'd done a poo.

We all laughed.

'Well done, Marco,' said Lorenzo's dad.

'I think he was talking to you,' Lorenzo's mom dangled a fresh diaper over the bowl of cauliflower in Lorenzo's dad's direction.

'I'll change him,' I said.

Lorenzo's dad took the diaper. 'Booooof,' he said, making a sound like a foot hitting a ball. 'Emilio takes the pass from Susanna. He juggles it over the head of the defender and passes it to his left wing.'

He tossed the diaper and I snatched it before it hit the bowl of pasta.

'Not a great pass, but a great save,' he said.

I leaned to one side and threw the diaper to Lorenzo who laughed.

'Ohhhhh,' said Lorenzo's dad, 'Now it's in the hands of a deadly striker. Will he pass or shoot?'

Lorenzo swung his arm up and threw it back to me.

'Enough,' said Lorenzo's mom. 'I don't want a diaper in the pasta. Even a clean one. Come, I'll help you, Rebecca.'

'She's the UG, Mamma,' said Lorenzo.

'When she's playing football she can be the UG but when she's inside she's going to be Rebecca. Just like you're my little Lorenzino ...' She reached out and pinched Lorenzo's cheek.

'Ok, Mamma. Ok.'

'Come now. Let's get the baby changed so we can all eat in comfort.'

She lifted Marco down and we took him to the changing table in the bathroom.

I lifted Marco up onto the changing table and handed him a small rattle with a rubber ring. He took it right away and started chewing.

His chubby legs wiggled in the air. I slipped off his comfy trousers and undid the old diaper.

I was surprised that such a small baby could make so much yellow poo.

I glanced up at Lorenzo's mom. She nodded. I wiped Marco's bum with the back of the diaper first, collecting as much loose poo as I could and I slipped a paper under him.

I folded the diaper quickly and Lorenzo's mom took it and placed it in a sealed bin on the side.

I pulled a baby wipe from the round container dispenser and rubbed Marco's bottom. It took three of them to get him clean.

'You're doing great,' said Lorenzo's mom.

I'd grabbed a clean diaper from the shelf over Marco's head, unfolded it and found the front. You can tell it's the front because it's got the design on it. I lifted Marco's feet and rolled them back. I slid the diaper under him. He kicked when I released his feet and looked up at me.

Lorenzo's mom reached out and shook the rattle a bit and that caught Marco's attention.

I opened the flaps on the diaper and folded the front over Marco's belly then taped it closed.

'Perfect, Rebecca. What a good job you did.'

'Thanks,' I said.

I slid Marco's trousers back up and Lorenzo's mom lifted him down. She sat him in the hall and let him crawl around.

She turned the water on in the faucet and we washed our hands.

'You know, Rebecca. If you need to talk about things, you can talk to me.'

She placed her hand on my shoulder.

I knew that if I started talking about things I would tell her everything. I'd tell her about my brothers and my Mom not moving from the couch. I'd tell her that I'd seen the woman from Social Services.

Everything was too much. I didn't want to say everything, so I said nothing.

'Let's go eat,' she said.

Marco crawled ahead of us into the kitchen. He pulled himself up beside Lorenzo who lifted him up and helped him back into the high chair.

We started eating.

'There's one more thing,' said Lorenzo's dad. 'If the meeting's still in session.'

'Sure,' said Lorenzo's mom.

He lifted a bag onto his lap and opened it. As soon as I saw it, I knew what it was.

A soccer jersey, just like Lorenzo's. He turned it for me to see. It was number 9. There were two letters printed over the number … UG.

I jumped up, took the shirt into my arms and hugged it. I pulled it on over my t-shirt.

Practice

Lorenzo and I practiced hard every day after we did our homework. Sometimes we did the first half of our homework, practiced and then finished off the rest of our lessons.

The team practiced on Thursdays. Lorenzo's dad, Coach Emilio, was like a different person when he was coaching. He was still nice, but he was way stricter. When he said something everyone on the team listened.

Coach Emilio made us do lots of drills. He said that it was important to practice the right things so that we improve faster.

'When you play, you improve your game, but it's during practice that you create new good habits,' he said. 'Then, you improve faster.'

'Ok,' he said, dropping multi-colored cones in a line across the field. 'Inside, outside, right,' he shouted to us. That meant that we had to dribble the ball using only our right foot all the way along the line.

'Work your way through, nice and slow. Don't miss a cone or you start again. Let's go.'

If the ball shot off in one direction or another, we had to run back into the line. It was hard, but I learned that it was better to go slow, even if it felt too slow than to rush it and have to start again.

'The fastest way to get fast is to practice slow!' shouted Coach Emilio.

I didn't really believe him. None of us did, but he was the coach, so we got in line.

It was as if he became Coach Emilio in the same way that I became UG when I played.

On the field, I was all UG. The way I handled the ball, the way I moved and talked, the way I pointed and passed. I liked being that person. UG knew what to do, Rebecca wasn't always so sure.

I thought we'd have to do inside, outside, left, but Coach had set up a line of cones just outside the goalie box on the left hand side of the field.

'Now we're going to do the chippy,' he said. 'UG you run into position. I pass the ball back to you. You chip the ball up and over to attack.'

The rest of the team lined up on the right side and Coach kicked the ball to me. I kicked with one touch, up and over to Pietro who shot, then Lorenzo and then one after another, again and again. We went through the entire team at least three times before we changed sides, and it was Aldo's turn.

'In a game, you might do this once or twice. So we make it count,' said Coach.

Aldo was great at passing. It was as if he could see where a player was headed, and he timed his kick perfectly.

I was so busy watching every pass he made, that I didn't notice when it was my turn. One of the guys nudged me and I sprinted towards the goal.

Coach tossed him the ball and Aldo chipped it so that it landed right in front of me. I blasted it into the net.

When we finished technical practice, we played small three on three matches. Lots of contact with the ball, passing and running.

It made you think differently and play by instinct.

It also brought out everyone's personality. Pietro, the hot shot, Lorenzo the striker, Aldo the elegant, UG the hustler.

That's how I thought of myself in matches. I would go anywhere, do anything and push myself as hard as I could every time I had the ball or had the chance of getting the ball.

Coach Emilio said I had the 'hustle,' and that was true.

I don't think any of us wanted practice to end. But parents began popping up on the sidelines. That meant it would be soon time to go home.

I took a step back towards the field.

Cars backed away from the parking lot. Lorenzo jogged to fetch equipment. I ran out too and helped him gather everything together. Cones, balls, Little Mario's water bottle that he left on the side of the goal post.

Someone left something behind every week.

We packed the gear into the back of the car and hopped in. I sat in the back seat wishing I could have stayed on the field all night. I wished I could live in the field house where they kept the equipment. I could set up a small kitchen and take care of the gear. It would be perfect.

I rubbed my hand on my head, feeling the soft fuzz. I rubbed behind my ears and then up to the crown of my head and back down again.

I could hear the sound the rubbing made. Lorenzo and Coach probably couldn't hear my hand moving at all. But to me it was soothing and peaceful.

I leaned against the sack of soccer balls that was on the passenger seat beside me. They smelled of grass and the outdoors.

I loved that smell.

Home Practice

I practiced even when I wasn't practicing.

I snuck downstairs to the basement for fifteen minutes of juggling before my brothers woke up. The basement was cool in the summer and warm in the winter. Perfect for early morning training. I had cleared out a spot and laid out an ugly old green shag carpet that reminded me of grass. It was my mini practice field.

There was lots of unused stuff in the basement like a black plastic bag filled with old shoes. I looked inside once and they didn't look at all like anything Mom would ever wear. How did they make it into the house? There were lots of parts of broken things, especially old toys. There was a red and yellow oven that I got as a kid. And a hockey table with movable guys that the boys fought over for a few years. If you pulled and twisted metal rods that stuck out of the sides, you could get the small plastic players to shoot. I don't think that it ever made it upstairs. I suppose my mom figured that they'd come down and play on it here. Now it was covered with other old junk.

A few armchairs with smelly striped cushions acted as buffers so that the ball wouldn't shoot off if I lost control.

I draped an old curtain over the hockey table and used it as a mini goal when I felt the urge to shoot.

There were a few other ripped plastic bags with old clothes sticking out of them like the stuffing on the scarecrow in the Wizard of Oz.

I used those as camouflage to cover my mini playing field when I was done, just in case my brothers ever noticed my set-up down there. I didn't want them messing with my spot.

It only took a second to move the bags onto the chairs and to pile them back onto the floor again when I was done.

I never bothered to go through the bags, but I figured that they must have belonged to my father when he still lived here.

Is it odd that Mom had kept his old shirts in sacks in the basement?

Why hadn't she just thrown them out or given them to charity?

I would have chucked them. But at least now, I had put them to good use as easy to move ground cover.

My spot was big enough for me to do push ups, sit-ups and deep knee bends when I was finished with my fifteen minutes of juggling. I did three sets of twenty.

Then I stretched with my arms up as high as I could reach and bent down low, swinging my arms. It made my body feel alive.

When I finished, I pulled the bags back into disguise position and got ready for school.

Practice made me strong. Practicing every day made me feel invincible. No one can keep up when you work at something every day. If you do something every day, then you don't get tired when the going gets tough.

In the middle of the second half of the match when everyone is sucking wind, you can be strong. When you've run as fast and hard as you thought you could, it's the strength from the deep knee bends that gets you through.

I was easing my way up the stairs when I heard someone in the kitchen. I continued up the stairs and felt the wood creaking under my feet. Mom stood in her robe making coffee. Her hair and make-up were already done.

'Morning,' she said. She placed a hot mug off coffee on the table and then pulled down a breakfast bowl from the cupboard for me.

'Morning,' I said. I opened the door to the freezer and fetched a bag of blueberries. I poured them into the bowl. She pulled the milk from the fridge.

'Up early?' she said.

'No,' I said. 'This is my normal time.'

'Of course,' she said. 'Early for me.' She forced a smile and sipped her coffee.

'Yeah,' I said. 'I suppose.'

I wondered what she wanted. She hardly ever got up early in the morning. And when she did, she hardly ever talked except for telling us to hurry up and get ready for school.

'How's it going?' she said.

'Good,' I said.

'I mean, with after school and everything,' she said.

'Good,' I said.

What did she want me to say?

'I mean you don't mind going to Lorenzo's,' she said.

'No. I don't mind,' I said.

Should I tell her that I love it? Should I tell her that I'd rather go to Lorenzo's than to come here every day for the next 365 days a year, including Christmas and my birthday?!

'I could try to pick you up some time after school and we could do something,' she said.

'Like what?'

'We could … I don't know, go to the mall, shop, or get our hair done.'

She stopped short. Her eyes glued to my bald scalp. I was shaving in the shower every third day now.

I saw her chin quiver, like Charles Ingalls on 'Little House on the Prairie.' His chin quivered whenever he was about to cry, especially if something happened to Laura. It was one of Mom's favorite shows. We used to watch the reruns together.

'I'm ok,' I said.

She handed me my cereal. I pulled out the milk and poured it on top. I plucked out a milk covered blueberry and popped it into my mouth.

'It would be nice to do something together,' she said.

Hmmmmm … Would it? Would it really be nice to do something together?

My mind raced for things that I'd like to do with Mom. It was too cold for the beach or for the amusement park. She didn't really like the rides anyway.

'We could go to the movies,' I said. 'I like the movies.'

The good thing about the movies is that you don't have to talk. You're not even allowed to. It's the perfect mother/daughter activity.

'The movies?' she said, as if she were weighing the idea. 'We could,' she said.

I knew by the way that she said 'we could' that we would never do it. She would never pick me up after school on a Friday or look through the paper together the night before to choose a movie. We didn't like the same types of films anyway.

I told myself that I'd rather practice than go to a movie with mom. But that wasn't exactly true.

I ladled a heaping spoonful of cereal and frozen blueberries into my mouth and crunched.

Thursday

I slept at home, but I didn't live at home.

Every night at bedtime Lorenzo and his dad would walk with me through the neighborhood, over the grass of the abandoned lot, past the lilac bushes and they would leave me on the top of the small hill that sloped down to the back of our house.

They waited until I opened the back door and waved before turning back home themselves.

The TV was on, the boys sitting on the floor watching Thursday night's fights and car chases.

Mom lay on the couch in her peach-colored bathrobe. It was hard to tell if she was watching the program or just staring into the screen.

I walked through the kitchen, turned right, walked down the stairs and leaned my backpack against the wall.

I hung my practice clothes on the laundry line in the basement, so that they would dry out during the night.

I came back upstairs and went into the bathroom. I took a shower every night, mainly because I was always a bit sweaty and muddy after practicing soccer with Lorenzo, but also because it was easier than trying to get shower time in the morning.

There was always plenty of hot water at night too, so I stayed there a long time. I could shave my head and I even started brushing my teeth in the shower.

It felt a bit odd the first time I got the idea because I had to reach out and get my toothbrush while I was all wet and then the toothpaste too. But now, I just set them on the side of the tub and pick them up when I'm ready to brush.

It's refreshing to brush your teeth in the running water. I also like to watch the toothpaste splat down on the bottom of the tub when I spit it out. I wonder if anyone else brushes their teeth in the shower. I bet they do.

It's warm and cozy in the water and once I start showering, I want to stay in as long as I can.

I finished brushing my teeth and rinsed the brush under the showerhead, cupping my hands to make sure it was totally clear of toothpaste. A cloud of steam seeped out into the hall as I walked out of the bathroom and my skin was soft and warm.

The TV flickered in the dark. I don't remember when I stopped saying goodnight. It didn't feel like there was any reason to say it anymore. My brothers never answered me anyway. And the most I got out of Mom was a mumble.

I looked over into the flickering greenish light from the TV and watched my brothers as they watched their show. I looked down at the top of Mom's head. Her hair swirled around the paisley couch pillow.

She didn't move much.

I don't know what time she went to bed. But at least I didn't find her sleeping on the couch in the morning when I got up to get ready.

I figured that was a good thing.

Even though our couch is pretty comfy, I've slept on it a few, and it's hard to get a good night's sleep.

I walked through the living room and wondered if there'd come a time when I wouldn't notice them at all. I reached the stairs and went up to my room.

No one came into my room anymore, ever, except me. I liked it that way. I could keep things exactly the way I liked them.

I had a 'Do Not Enter' sign on my door. And I meant it. My brothers used to barge in sometimes when they were attacking me, but because I didn't get home until after mom they didn't have the chance to anymore.

I wondered if they fought with each other when I wasn't there.

The more research I did for my history of soccer project, the more pictures I had of soccer players on my wall.

I could rest at night surrounded by greatness. And I needed rest because practice was hard.

Lorenzo and I have been working on pace and passing. His Dad says that if we can keep up a strong pace and pass then we will be unstoppable.

I'd been practicing with the team on Thursdays. We were getting ready for a full day of soccer on Saturday. A daylong tournament held at the high school.

Lorenzo's dad said there would be lots of teams there from all over the state. Our team came in third last year and he said that we have a chance to win it this year.

I felt nervous. I'd never played in a tournament before. We were going to have to face the Wild Cats again. That made me nervous too. They were good, and we had already lost to them once.

I wanted to ask Mom to come and watch me play, but I knew that

Kenny and David both had baseball every Saturday, so I didn't ask her or tell her about it.

I figured I'd just get up and head over to Lorenzo's on Saturday morning like usual.

That night I dreamt that I was playing in a match and running for all I was worth. I fell into a hole and hit the bottom. I couldn't run. I couldn't even move.

But the worst thing about the dream was that the hole was so small that I couldn't even swing my foot to kick.

If you can't kick then there's no way out.

The Movies

The smell of pancakes wafted down the stairs right in the middle of my second set of sit-ups. Blueberry pancakes were my absolute favorite breakfast.

We never ate them on a weekday, ever. There was never enough time.

A strange thought hit me - what if I overslept and it was actually Saturday and the tournament was already starting while I was downstairs doing my normal routine?

I was pretty sure it was only Friday, but the smell of pancakes sent a shiver of panic through me.

I abandoned my last set of exercises and dashed upstairs.

Mom stood by the stove in her robe, hair and make-up complete.

'What day is it?' I asked in a quick breath.

'Good morning,' she said. 'I'm making pancakes.'

'What day is it, mom?'

'They're blueberry. Your favorite.'

'Is it Saturday?'

'It's Friday, Rebecca.'

'Oh,' I said. 'It smelled like a Saturday.'

'No, only Friday.'

I had the strange urge to fetch my bowl and cereal like usual. It felt odd to break the routine. But I set the table instead. Butter, maple syrup, silverware and four plates.

'Should I fetch Kenny and David?' I said.

'In a sec,' said Mom, stacking the last four pancakes on the large serving platter. 'I was thinking that if you'd like we could go to the movies tonight, like you suggested.'

'Really?' I asked.

'Yeah. Just you and me. Katherine said that she could take the boys tonight. Would you like that?'

'I … uh … guess so,' I said.

She actually did want to go to the movies.

'We have to call Lorenzo's mom,' I said.

'I'll do that,' said Mom.

'What do you want to see?'

'I don't know,' she said. 'We'll find something.'

'Ok, then,' I said.

'Why don't you call the boys?'

It had been weeks since I'd called them, but they appeared at the top of the stairs like they used to, blinking their eyes.

'What?' said Kenny.

'What?' said David.

You could tell that they were brothers. They had the same tone, the same empty.

'Pancakes,' I said.

'Pancakes?' said Kenny.

'Pancakes?' said David.

'Yeah. Mom made pancakes.'

'What day is it?' said David.

'It's Friday,' I said. 'Let's go, they're getting cold.' I left them there and went back into the kitchen. Mom had filled glasses of milk. The boys came down and sat in their places.

'You made pancakes,' said David.

'Yes,' said Mom. 'I feel like we all need some pancakes.'

'I love pancakes,' said David.

'I know,' said Mom.

'Me too,' said Kenny quickly. 'I love them more than anything.'

'I like them most,' said David.

'No way,' said Kenny.

Mom interrupted, 'Boys, I've spoken to Katherine and she said she'll pick you up at school and you can go over to Michael's tonight for a sleep over.'

'Do we have to, Mom? Michael's boring,' said Kenny. 'He always wants to play war games.'

'I thought you liked those kinds of games,' said Mom. 'You're always on the computer.'

'Not on the computer,' said Kenny. 'Like with little plastic guys. No one plays with plastic guys anymore. Boring.'

'I'm sure you can find something to do. Watch a film or something.'

'I'll only go if I can take the iPad with me,' said Kenny.

'You're not allowed to have it at school,' said Mom.

'I won't have it at school. I mean, I'll have it, but I promise that I won't play with it until I get to Kenny's.'

'What's she going to do?' asked David with a nod in my direction before stuffing his mouth with a forkful of maple-syrup-dripping-pancake.

'We're having a girls' night,' said Mom.

'A girls' night?' said David. 'What's that?'

'We're going to dinner and a movie.'

'Unfair!' shouted Kenny.

'Why can't we go to the movies?' asked David.

'Because it's a girls' night and that means that it's only for girls"

'That's not fair,' said Kenny.

'Totally NOT fair,' said David.

'You can watch a film at Michael's,' she said.

'It's not fair. Because we can't have a boys' night!' said Kenny.

'You can,' said Mom. 'Another time.'

'No! We can't!'

'Of course you can,' said Mom.

'NO!' shouted Kenny. 'Who's going to take us?'

Mom was trying so hard. She was being so patient. I felt bad for her. She floated there for a moment … alone, trembling. Even the strands of her hair shook. They looked like tiny branches sticking out from a cactus, all dry, and brown, and delicate.

Kenny stuffed his face with a wedge of pancake. David licked syrup off his fingers and downed a large swig of milk.

The sound of their squishing and slurping made me clench my teeth. I hated it, that they had a point. Who could take them to the movies on a boys' night? They didn't have a dad there to help them improve their swing or to shoot hoops in the backyard.

I pictured Lorenzo with his dad. He taught us small things that you don't learn in normal practice like the different ways you hold your foot when you kick to pass or kick to shoot. He taught us how to head fake and juggle. He taught us how to teach ourselves. How to practice alone.

'You have each other,' I said finally. 'You have each other to do stuff with. You're the two boys in the family and we're the two girls.'

Mom reached out and took my hand.

The tremble in her cheeks solidified from soft wobbly jello to warm red skin. Her hair softened in the morning light. Her eyes softened too.

She reached further and stroked from the top of my head to the back of my neck. She held her hand there for a moment, bending over the table.

I liked the feel of her hand, but then it felt awkward and noticed the way her robe folded just above her un-eaten pancake. She pulled up just in time, moving her hand from my neck, over my shoulder and back across the table.

'Can I have another pancake?' said David.

'Please,' said Mom.

'Please,' repeated David.

'Sure,' she said. She passed the serving platter and placed it in front of him. He jabbed the last pancake and glanced back and forth to me and Kenny.

'Does anyone want to share?' said Mom.

David repeated, 'does anyone want to share?' so quietly that it was nearly impossible to hear his voice.

'I'm good,' I said.

'It's still unfair,' said Kenny in a small voice.

Popcorn & Pizza

Movie popcorn is always best on Fridays.

And those first few bites, when you stick your tongue into the top of the carton and pluck out a few pieces taste best.

I was used to people looking at me now. My baldness made me stand out. But Mom hadn't been out with me since I'd shaved off my hair and I could tell she was nervous.

It was a relief that I didn't see anyone I knew from school.

Why didn't I want to be seen with my mom? I don't know, but I didn't.

She's not embarrassing or gross or anything. She's normal. Better than average, at least once she's got her face on.

No one stares at her when she walks around town. The girl in the ticket booth didn't look at her and neither did the one at the concession stand. They looked at me and then glanced up at her as if to say … 'Is there anything wrong with her?'

I suppose people wonder if I'm a cancer patient. Some moms in the waiting area gave her a sympathetic smile. People have no idea. Does anyone actually want sympathy anyway?

I think sympathy sucks.

When someone gives you sympathy, it makes you feel worse and it makes them feel worse, like there's something really wrong with them.

Like if you're injured in practice the last thing you want is someone cooing and crooning over you. All you need is an ice pack and a bandage. At least that's all I need.

Those sympathetic eyes were driving me crazy and making Mom feel worse than she probably already did to have a daughter like me.

I handed her the box, and pulled up the hood of my hoodie to cover my head. Mom took a bite or two of my popcorn. I noticed that her hands looked pudgy even though the rest of her wasn't fat or anything.

We went in to find our seats.

I like those moments when you first sit down in a cinema and get the feel of your seat. Put your drink in the holder, balance the popcorn on your lap, lean back, and make that spot a little cozy.

'I'm glad we're here,' said Mom.

'Yeah. Me too,' I said. I smiled at her and offered her popcorn. She took a few pieces and I noticed her hands again.

'Your hands look strange, Mom,' I said.

'Yes,' she said, stretching them out. 'I'm a bit swollen these days. It's nothing.' She examined her own fingers a bit longer before folding them into her lap.

The ads came on and we stopped talking. Then trailers for upcoming films, and then the film.

People have different reasons for going to the movies. To feel like superheroes. To escape their normal lives. Girls go with boys to hold hands in safety. Boys go with girls just to hold hands.

I went with Mom to be close to her. I finished up my popcorn after the first fifteen minutes. I felt my shoulder against hers and reached out and looped my arm through hers.

It was a musical about a family who live a crazy life on a Greek Island. It was kind of ok.

I watched for a while and then thought of my tournament the next morning. Then I watched a bit more and thought more about soccer. It's kind of crazy how things keep popping into your head again and again. Either good things or bad things.

I must have played in five matches by the time the movie was done.

'Do you want to go to the Country Kitchen?' asked Mom.

The Country Kitchen used to be my favorite restaurant when I was about five or six. Mostly because they had the best banana splits.

'No, thanks.' I said.

'How about a pizza?'

Why is telling the truth so hard sometimes? Telling someone something that they don't want to hear. I know that Mom didn't want to hear about my tournament and I didn't want to talk about it. I just wanted to get home and visualize the game.

'We could share a large mushroom and pepperoni,' said Mom.

She said it in a nice voice, and we had just sat next to one another for an hour and a half, and I didn't want her to feel bad, so I said, 'Ok.'

We walked towards the car. She reached in her purse and her keys jiggled.

'I have to get up early,' I said. 'Should we get a takeaway?'

'It's Saturday tomorrow,' she said.

I didn't answer.

'We can get takeaway,' she said.

'Great.'

She went around to her side of the car. I got in the passenger seat.

The pizza place was on the way home, so I called ahead and ordered while mom drove. When I hung up I looked over at Mom and said, 'ten minutes,' in an Italian accent copying the pizza guy.

We always joked about 10 minutes when we ordered pizza because they said the same thing every time. Ten minutes.

Mom laughed and repeated, 'ten minutes,' and waved her hand in the air. 'Whatever you want. I'll give it to you in ten minutes. Ok?' She joked.

Mom was actually funny when she talked with an Italian accent. It was nice to see her silly.

We parked in front of the pizzeria. There was a liquor store next door. She handed me twenty dollars, 'you go in and get the pizza. I'm going to go in next door for a second.'

The pizza was ready when I came in. The guy behind the counter always recognized me. He smiled. 'A large! Just for you? You going to eat the whole thing yourself?'

'No, my mom's going to eat some too,' I said.

'What about your brothers? You usually get a plain pepperoni too.'

'We're having a girl's night. Just me and Mom.'

I handed him the bill and he handed it right back and then slid the warm brown cardboard box across the counter.

Then he lifted out two pastries. And placed them in a small box.

'Here,' he said. 'For you and your mom. On the house.'

'Really?' I said.

'Yes, yes! You're on my son Pietro's soccer team. You have a big tournament tomorrow. No?'

'Yes!' I said.

I was glad Mom hadn't come in.

'You're Pietro's Dad?'

'Yes. Yes. He tells me you are an excellent player.'

'Really?' I said.

'Yes. Yes. Tonight you eat pizza and tomorrow you play like an Italian.'

'Thanks,' I said.

'You're welcome.'

I lifted the pizza box and the small pastry box slid on top like an ice skater. I had to balance to make sure it didn't fly off. Pietro's dad saw me adjust it.

'Quick reflex!' he said. 'It's good in a soccer player. Ciao!'

'Ciao!' I said as I backed out the door.

I rested the pizza on the front of the car, opened the door, grabbed the pizza, got in and felt the warm box on my lap. Then I thought, what about the change? How could I explain that the pizza was on the house and that it was because I was playing in the tournament tomorrow?

I slipped the twenty bucks into my pocket. Maybe I could go to my bank at home and give her change later on. She might not even think about it.

Mom opened the back door, placed her wine on the floor and then sat in the driver's seat again. She glanced over at the extra box. 'Ahhh, you had enough left for a pastry too. What did you get?'

She reached over and opened the smaller box. 'Cannoli. I love those. Great.'

The pizza was hot and warm so that my whole lap tingled. Meanwhile, the twenty-dollar bill was burning a hole in my pocket.

Mom started the engine and we were soon home. It was strange to be in the house when the boys weren't there. It felt like a different place.

First of all, it was quiet. Too quiet.

I looked at Mom and Mom looked at me. I placed the pizza on the counter. I love the smell when you first open the box. I bent over it and took a long, deep whiff.

Mom was looking at me when I closed the lid. She placed her bottle of wine on the counter beside her keys.

'Should I set up in the living room?' I said.

I took a few leaping steps and flicked on the TV. The sound immediately comforted me and made the house feel lived-in. I scrolled through the listings and clicked on 'The Pirates of the Caribbean.' Pirates for me, and Johnny Depp for Mom.

Mom poured me a glass of milk and a glass of wine for herself.

I fetched the box and plates. She took her spot on the couch and I sat on the floor, but leaned up against the couch too so that my shoulder was against Mom's calf.

We each took a slice. I sipped my milk and she sipped her wine.

Saturday in the Park

I woke early. Excited. I'd be playing a whole day of soccer and I was ready to go. I hopped out of bed and slid into my clothes.

As I opened the door to my room, I got the feeling that something was wrong. I hadn't heard it with the door closed, but now I heard the soft sound of the TV with the volume down low.

I eased down the stairs, hoping NOT to see her. I had imagined a quick breakfast and exit. But there she was, on the couch exactly where I had left her the night before when I went to bed ... Mom.

I stopped on the third step from the bottom. I needed a change of plan. I'd have to skip my normal blueberry and cereal breakfast.

I decided that if I were really, really quiet I could sneak past her, grab a piece of fruit and get out the door.

I took the last three steps real slow, one at a time and then I walked on my tiptoes by the couch.

That's when I made the mistake of looking again. Mom's cheek was drooped down. Her face looked like a rubber mask. I pictured her lying there all day, unable to move.

I couldn't just leave her without getting her a drink. Her eyes were slightly open. They blinked in slow motion, like they did on the doll that I used to play with when I was small. Baby Care Kim. If you gave her a bottle her eyes would slowly close and she'd fall asleep. She even gurgled like a baby. I thought that's the way they actually sounded when you fed them until I got the chance to feed Marco. Then I knew that real babies don't sound like Baby Care Kim at all.

'Mom,' I whispered.

Her chest rose like she was taking in air to speak but then a long sigh came out instead of a word.

'Mom,' I whispered a bit louder. 'I was thinking of having breakfast. Can I get you a drink?'

Her head moved slightly up and down. If I had blinked, I would have missed it. But I knew that she must be thirsty.

I went into the kitchen. I started filling a glass with water for her but then thought that maybe she needed something with some substance to it, so I put the kettle on for tea.

I figured if I made honey tea with lots of milk then that would make her feel a bit better.

I filled my bowl with cereal and blueberries while the water was boiling. Might as well eat because breakfast is important if you're going to play soccer all day.

I decided on a cup of honey tea for myself too. I set two mugs on the counter and spooned a heaping portion of honey in each and plopped a teabag in each. I poured the boiling water in half full and stirred until the honey dissolved then I filled the rest with cold milk.

I waited a minute and pulled the tea bags out, wrapping them with the cord around the spoon and squeezing out the warm liquid from them.

I sipped mine to make sure it wasn't too hot. Perfect. I carried Mom's mug into her and kneeled in front of the couch holding the mug.

'Mom, mom,' I whispered. 'I've made some honey tea for you.'

Her eyes opened three quarters and she jacked herself up onto her arms. She seemed like the weakest person alive. The flesh of her arms trembled under the weight, but soon she was sitting.

She swung her legs down onto the floor. I'd seen pictures of Mom when she was a girl and played field hockey. She used to have strong fast legs like mine but now they were puffy in the ankles and around her knees.

Her fingers wrapped around the teacup. She sipped. There's something about tea that just makes you feel better. She forced a smile. 'Thanks,' she said.

'You're welcome,' I said.

'It's Saturday. You're up early,' she said.

'Yes. I'm headed over to Lorenzo's,' I said.

Something inside of me didn't want to tell her about the tournament. I wasn't afraid that she would stop me from going, it was more like I didn't want her to think about me going. Maybe I didn't want her to think about me at all. I just wanted to go.

'At this hour?' she asked.

'Yeah,' I said. 'They'll be up,' I paused. 'Because of the baby.'

'Of course,' she said, taking a longer chug. 'Good tea,' she said.

I stood.

'I should have my breakfast. They're expecting me by 7.30.' I said.

'You like going there,' she said, her eyes focused on the tea, but it sounded a bit like she was asking at the same time.

'Yeah,' I said. 'It's ok.'

I went to the kitchen and fetched my tea and bowl of cereal. I brought them back into the living room and knelt in front of the coffee table.

Mom watched me eat.

I shoveled in muesli and blueberries as efficiently as I could, washing them down with warm tea at intervals.

I was nearly done when Mom said, 'it would be nice if you were home for supper.'

'But we won't be back until after six,' I said.

I saw the flicker in her eyes and knew I'd made a mistake.

'After six,' she said.

'Yes,' I said. 'There's a soccer tournament today,' I said.

'Oh,' she said. 'Is Lorenzo playing?' she asked.

A flash of anger shot up my spine. I could have just said 'yes,' and technically I wouldn't have been lying because Lorenzo and I played on the same team, but instead I said. 'We're both playing.'

'Both playing?'

'Yes. We're on the same team.'

I stood up, picked up my bowl, sucked down the last bit of tea in my mug and brought them into the kitchen.

I dropped them in the sink just hard enough for them not to break. I could have smashed them, but that would mean that I'd have to stay home longer to clean them up.

I turned on the water full steam but didn't really rinse them well.

I dried off my hands and stood in the doorway. Mom hadn't moved a muscle.

'Ok, bye,' I said.

Mom mouthed the word 'bye,' but I didn't hear a sound. She said it exactly as loud as Kenny spoke the few times that he was made to apologize for something.

I strode to the hall door, swung it open and slammed it behind me. I stuffed my gear into my backpack and opened the door.

I walked out into the early Saturday morning fresh air, turned around and grabbed the handle to the door. I slammed that one closed too, so hard that the house shook behind me.

I couldn't wait to get to the field and kick that ball.

Making Me Wait

The high school sport grounds were transformed into a carnival of soccer. I don't know how many teams were there, but everyone had their own colored jerseys with names and numbers on the back.

My cleats clicked as we crossed the running track that encircled the playing fields.

Temporary goals had been wheeled in and the larger fields had been broken down into four smaller ones. That meant that eight teams could play at once.

The members of our team met up on the right just after the entrance gate. Some of the parents of kids that I'd been practicing with came along too. I recognized a few of those who hung out on the sidelines during practice. I don't think that I'd ever spoken to any of them, so I figured that they didn't even know who I was.

We walked towards the registration table and Lorenzo's dad signed us in. Most of the team members crowded in around the table. I hung back with Lorenzo.

Soccer balls flew in all directions. Some players juggled, while others kicked long passes to one another. Dads and moms mostly stood around, but a few of them were kicking, passing and juggling too. We were assigned a field for our first match and we stuck together as a group, heading to the field on the far left by the football goal post. We stacked our bags under it and started warming up.

I had been a bit nervous as we were driving to the tournament but now there were so many players, parents, whistles, coaches and referees running around that it was impossible to be nervous any more.

It was time to play.

We huddled around Lorenzo's dad. 'Ok,' he said. 'Today we play a lot of football. It's a long day, you're going to be running a lot. Don't worry. When you do run, I want you to run without the ball. If you pass the ball then the ball moves fast … but if you run with the ball, the ball moves slow. So we pass and run … pass and run. When we run, we get in position. We pass, run, position. Pass, run, position. What do we do?'

We all shouted, 'pass, run, position.'

'Perfect, that's how we win. Ok, let's go.'

We played twenty-minute halves. The first half felt more like twenty seconds than twenty minutes. The score was zero - zero. We had a short pause. Lorenzo's dad said, 'Ok, you're playing good. No mistakes. That's good. Now it's time to make some plays. Widen out to the sides a bit more. UG, Aldo open up like the jaws of a dragon along the lines and then pass in to Lorenzo and Pietro. You're the fire. The dragon attack.'

I intercepted the ball about two minutes into the second half, mid-field center. I was about to pass straight up to Pietro, who was only a few steps in front of me. It wasn't a good angle and then I pictured the dragon. Instead of kicking it to Pietro I flipped the ball out towards the sideline. I chased it out to my own left hopping over the leg of the opposing mid-fielder. I dashed to the ball just before it reached the sideline.

I knew where Lorenzo was, almost without looking. I glanced up at him just as my left foot hit the ball. It sailed over the heads of the defenders directly in front of him on the right side of the field.

Perfect.

He shot. One touch. And we were up 1 - 0.

'Bellisima!' shouted Lorenzo's dad from the sideline.

I got the ball a few times over the next fifteen minutes and tried for a repeat but couldn't get the timing right. I saw Aldo trying too. He made a few excellent passes to Pietro, but the other team's defenders clamped down fast.

That entire first match was easy for our goalie, Little Mario. He didn't have to make one save. We won by one goal.

I was glad for that.

We had a short pause after the first match. I wondered who we would play next. I wondered who else would win their first matches.

Winners got to stay at the same fields. We didn't have to lug our gear or find a new place to sit. So it felt like we had the home field advantage as we started the second match. Strange how quickly you get used to a place.

Just before our second match was about to begin, I saw the WildCats' coach walk up to Lorenzo's dad. They chatted for a moment or two.

The WildCats' coach motioned to the field and pointed. I swear he was pointing at me, so I looked away, just in time too, because Aldo had passed the ball in my direction. I got it, pulled it down, into control and passed it back.

The referee came to the center of the field. One of the guys kicked the ball to him and he popped it up. I hadn't looked over at him until that second but then recognized him at once.

'Mr. McCartney!' I said.

He winked at me. 'Hey there.'

Lorenzo and I walked closer. 'Hi, Mr. McCartney,' said Lorenzo.

'So you two are on the same team, at school and on the soccer pitch?' he said 'That's great.'

'Yes,' I said. 'And I didn't know you were a ref.'

'I am a referee for today's tournament, but I'm actually the coach for the varsity high school soccer team.'

'You are?' Lorenzo and I asked at the same time.

'Yep!' said Mr. McCartney. 'Middle school history teacher by day and soccer coach by night.'

'I didn't know that,' I said.

'Me neither,' said Lorenzo.

'So you'd both better do a great job on that paper that you're working on for my class because I know everything about the history of soccer.' He smiled.

'Everything?' I said.

'Well, everything is probably an exaggeration. I'm sure you two will do great. Now it's time to get this match started.'

We stepped back.

Mr. McCartney blew his whistle and Lorenzo met the captain of the opposing team in the middle. They flipped a coin for first possession and the ball was soon in play.

I wanted to score a goal so badly that I nearly missed the first pass that Mario kicked forward. I managed to catch up to the ball just in time to make a weak pass to Aldo, who took excellent control of the ball and we advanced on our first attack.

Pietro barely felt the ball on his foot as he passed to Lorenzo, who was immediately tackled by a large back. It was a good play even though we didn't get a shot off.

Lorenzo's dad shouted from the sidelines, 'Bene! Bene! Pass, Run, Position.

The other team's midfielder ran to the center with the ball. He was a bit off balance, but our backs were doing a great job defending the strikers. He shot at our goal. Little Mario jumped into action and smashed the ball away.

Their striker was good and managed to get a second shot off before we were ready. He blasted it into the upper right hand corner of our goal.

I felt our whole team breathe out a sigh of frustration.

The only happy one was Lorenzo's dad who clapped and cheered from the sidelines.

'Bene! Bene! That was good football. Now we can stop worrying and start playing too.'

I'd grown used to the way our coach was. He always found a way to lift us up. He always found something good to say.

When the ball was back in play, Pietro kicked it back to Aldo. Aldo passed to me and I lobbed it across the field to Lorenzo.

But that back from the other team was in his face again. This time Lorenzo passed it back to Aldo.

I ran up the middle. Position, I thought. The ball dropped right in front of me. The defenders had focused on Pietro and Lorenzo. I was within my range. I'd blasted hundreds of balls from this distance in practice.

Lorenzo's dad yelled, 'Shoot, UG!'

My foot was already in motion and I booted that ball with such a snap that it curved out to the right and spun into the back of the net.

My first GOAL!

Now we were tied!

As soon as I scored, we went back to defensive mode and neither team made any headway before half time.

Lorenzo's dad knelt in front of us. 'UG! Good goal. Your first goal in competition, eh?'

I nodded.

'Congratulations. You break the ice!'

I smiled.

'But for the team, it came too easy. They score a goal, you start playing football. You score a goal, you stop playing football. I know you want to win. But to win at football you have to stop thinking about winning at football. You have to play football. Forget win! Play! Smile like Pele! Run, Pass … Run some more. Position! Now let's go!'

We broke the huddle and I could see that Mr. McCartney had been listening. He walked beside me. 'That's one heck of a good coach you have there,' he said to me.

'Thanks. I said. It's Lorenzo's dad.'

Mr. McCartney started the second half and we were off. This time both teams were running and it felt like practice. When Pietro got the ball, he did a few too many hotshot moves before trying to pass. That gave the defender time to cover him, but it made me laugh.

He got so stuck that he had to pass back to me with a heel kick. But I was ready, because he always did that in practice. I barely touched the ball before kicking it to Aldo who loved to dribble center. He did.

Pietro rolled off his defender and Lorenzo cut around the side. Aldo passed to Pietro, who shot. The back did his job and we had a corner.

Lorenzo's dad told us that he didn't want us diving in from behind on corners to head the ball like they do in the pros but Paul loved running in from behind and doing just that.

This time he did, the ball bounced to the left of the goalie into the net. Paul jumped up, running, lifting his shirt.

'Basta! Basta!' shouted Lorenzo's dad. But when we looked over at him, he smiled with his arms in the air. 'Bene! Bene!' He shouted now. 'Keep playing!'

We were still having fun and suddenly there were only two minutes left. I could see by the look in his eyes that Lorenzo was hungry to score.

He'd made a few good runs, but the defense player who covered him was brilliant. We were all back in our half of the field when I got the ball and started to break.

'Weave,' I shouted to Lorenzo. He ran in front of me. I passed him the ball and I crossed to the right as he passed back. I took about five steps at full speed and kicked the ball across to Lorenzo just before the defender towered over me.

Lorenzo was now facing the second defender. Lorenzo head-faked to the left, booted the ball to the right and was suddenly open. He shot into the upper left hand corner of the goal.

He turned, pointed at me and gave me the thumbs up.

The whistle blew. We won.

'Good match,' said Mr. McCartney to me and Lorenzo.

'Thanks!' we both said.

'Well, the tournament continues. Maybe I'll get a chance to see you play again in the finals!' Said Mr. McCartney.

'Yes!' I said.

He turned and approached Lorenzo's dad. I saw them shake hands but couldn't hear what they said. I could see Lorenzo's dad saying, 'Bene, bene. Thank you, thank you.'

I figured Mr. McCartney was telling him how awesome he thought we were.

I would have been better if the tournament had ended there.

Kicked

The Team from Fall River wore blood red jerseys and black shorts. Their coach shouted at them when it was time to take the field.

I glanced towards our small group of fans and recognized Pietro's dad from the pizzeria. He waved and gave me a thumbs up. His friendliness made me smile.

I turned my attention back to the start of the match.

Most of us hung back as Lorenzo and Pietro approached the ref and two of the other team's players for a coin toss.

It doesn't really matter which team gets the ball first in soccer, at least not as much as it does in other sports where the coin toss winner can decide to receive the ball first and then begin a charge.

Soccer is more fluid. Often, the ball changes sides many times before a team can build up a play or take advantage of the opposition's mistakes.

But their coach, a short curly haired man, flung his arms up in the air in anger at losing the toss. The ref turned towards the sideline and one of the boys from the other team jabbed Pietro with a quick, sharp kidney shot.

Pietro grabbed his side. The boys trotted off. I think I was the only one to see the cheap shot.

Lorenzo turned trotted over to Pietro. 'What's up?'

'He just hit me,' said Pietro.

I rushed forward.

'I saw it. He punched him,' I said.

'We'll have to keep an eye on that guy,' said Lorenzo.

The ref bounced the ball and blew his whistle to let us know that he wanted us to take our positions. I ran out towards the left.

Lorenzo stood over the ball. The ref blew and the match started. Lorenzo passed quickly to Pietro, who flicked the ball to Aldo. We were off.

Our teams were evenly matched and the ball changed hands a lot before we started to settle down and really play soccer.

Pietro had just kicked the ball into the goalie's hands and the guy who had jabbed him during the coin toss booked it in my direction. The goalie threw him the ball and he decided to take me on.

I'm not the best defender but I'd been practicing with Lorenzo and Pietro, who had the same hotshot attitudes as this guy. I learned to take charge and aim for the belly because you go wherever your belly goes. Tackle when you're close enough and don't get fooled by their tricks. I did that now and stole the ball.

I booted it away, when the player kicked me in the shin. I went down but my pass was good enough to reach Pietro who passed directly to Lorenzo.

Lorenzo made the most of the second that he had and shot up into the left hand corner of the goal. I lay curled up for a few seconds, then I rolled myself up. I jogged in place. He wasn't going to get me that easily. It was a good thing I had my shin guards.

The coach from the other team shouted at the boy, 'You lost that ball! You practically gave it to him!'

'It's a girl,' said the boy.

'A what?!' shouted the coach.

'A girl,' said the boy.

The ref was off retrieving the ball. And Lorenzo's dad was on the far side of the field.

'You lost the ball to a girl!' The coach looked over to me. 'Hey! Are you a girl?'

I didn't know what to say. I stood, silent.

The referee trotted back to the center of the field.

I turned away from the coach without answering but could feel him pacing back and forth on the sideline, watching me like some predator, trying to see if I were a boy or a girl.

I wasn't giving anything away. I made myself taller, stronger. The ball was in play.

One good thing about soccer is that there aren't a lot of time outs. Once the ball's in play then it's full on unless there's a penalty.

We made it to the first half 1-0. But it was mostly thanks to Little Mario's goal tending. He saved at least five shots that could have evened the score.

'What's happening out there?' asked Lorenzo's dad.

'They cheat,' grumbled Pietro.

'Yeah,' said Lorenzo. 'They grab and pull the whole time.'

'I've seen that they're physical.'

'One of the strikers kicked me,' I said.

'It's hard to play well and concentrate when you think someone's going to hit you. True. True. Ok. But the best we can do is to calm down. Focus on the game. I'll talk to the ref.'

'He's not calling anything,' said Aldo.

'It's like he's on their side,' said Pietro.

'He sucks,' said Lorenzo.

'Hey!' said Lorenzo's dad. 'We don't talk like that. When we talk bad, we play bad.'

'Ok,' said Lorenzo, sinking his head.

'Ok. You can beat this team. You're better at teamwork. We don't just hold tight. We play soccer. We're bold. We attack. Yes?'

'Yes!' we said.

'I'll be back in a second.' Lorenzo's dad stood and walked over to the referee. I saw him talking and motioning toward the other team.

The referee nodded, but I could tell he wasn't listening. He had that same look that Kenny got when you tried to say anything to him that he didn't want to hear. But Lorenzo's dad spoke patiently and then came back to the team.

'Let's play our best football. If we win this match, we make it to the semi-finals.'

We ran out, ready to play. Lorenzo beat a midfielder and headed towards a tall back, who looked like he was fifteen. The guy didn't even look like he was going for the ball and swept Lorenzo's legs sending him in a somersault through the air.

The referee didn't see, or didn't react to the foul. Play continued.

Lorenzo's dad rushed out on the field.

Lorenzo rolled on the ground holding his leg.

The coach from the other team called to the tall boy. 'It's ok, it doesn't matter.'

Lorenzo's dad jumped up. 'It doesn't matter! It doesn't matter! What's wrong with you?!'

The other team's coach said, 'I didn't mean that it doesn't matter that he's hurt …'

'What did you mean?! You play dirty. Your boys play dirty! This is not soccer!'

I'd never seen Lorenzo's dad raise his voice before. He turned back, reached down to Lorenzo and helped him up. Lorenzo started hobbling, but then shook it off.

Tension.

Lorenzo was on fire. Once the ball was back in play, he passed back to Aldo who kicked the ball to me. I rushed forward and we attacked. I was ready this time. I chipped the ball to Pietro and made a run towards the goal. He passed back. The defender rushed me.

He aimed for my knee. He raised his leg. I saw a flicker in his eyes … the same that my brothers had when they attacked. I hopped and kicked. Hard. I felt my toe sink into his calf muscle. The ball shot off in Pietro's direction. The boy crumpled to the grass. Down, down, down you go.

'Cheater,' I whispered.

I sunk back onto the green grass. I imagined it folding around me like my armchair at home. I gazed up at the clouds in the sky. It felt like I could see forever … at least until Mr. McCartney's face blocked my view. From his worried look, I suppose he thought I was dead or something.

'You ok?' he said.

'Yeah,' I said. 'I'm good.'

Lorenzo's dad appeared a moment later. They both helped me up. But I felt great.

The other guy wouldn't be kicking any more of our teammates for a while because he got kicked out of the game.

The ref finally made a good call.

Disqualified

We'd made it to the semi-finals. I scored two goals throughout the day. And all day, no one had really noticed me. Or at least no one had said anything about my being a girl, until we sat, watching.

It was our turn to sit out and watch a decider match, to see who we would be playing against in the semis. It was the team led by the WildCats' coach against a group of very tall, older looking boys. It was as if they'd gotten the basketball team to play soccer. Plus they were dressed in green stripes. We called them the Jolly Green Giants.

It was a strangely even match. The WildCats were quick and skillful and the Jolly Green Giants strong and powerful.

I wasn't sure who I'd rather face.

'Wow,' said Lorenzo. 'Those guys must be fourteen. They're huge.'

When they tackled, the smaller boys flew off in all directions and looked like small beetles spinning around in their black jerseys and matching shorts.

'Yeah, but their goalie sucks,' said Little Mario who was lying beside Lorenzo with his head resting on a ball. 'He's never in the right position.'

Just then one of the three brothers on the WildCats blasted a low hard shot along the grass into the left. The goalie dove, but the ball zipped past him before he hit the ground.

The WildCats' coach stood with his arms crossed, nodding, before barking out orders, 'Good! Now GET in position!'

His players scampered around and the ball was back in play.

I was staring at the coach. He kind of scared me. I wondered what it would be like to have a hard, mean Dad like that. Better not to have one at all.

Two men in red windbreakers carrying clip boards with papers that curled in the breeze walked up behind the WildCats' coach.

They said something to him and then he nodded again and pointed, across the field of play, directly at me.

My insides squirmed.

I looked away.

Had he seen that I was staring?

'Want to kick the ball around?' I said to Lorenzo.

'No,' he said. 'I want to watch.'

'You?'

'Nah,' said Little Mario.

I wanted to do something else, to get away from there, but there was nowhere to go to. I looked back behind me to see if there were any other teammates for me to latch onto.

I couldn't move.

I glanced back towards the field and the WildCats' coach and saw that the men in clipboards were gone. He was shouting at his players. I couldn't hear what he was saying.

Maybe he wasn't looking at me at all.

I looked behind me again. The men with clipboards were walking towards us with Lorenzo's dad.

I tried to ignore them. But I felt them standing behind me.

'UG,' said Lorenzo's dad softly. 'These men here, they want to talk to us.'

'Yes,' said one of the men in the red windbreakers, 'we were told …'

Lorenzo's dad put his hand up. 'Please, please … we're a team and I would like to talk as a team.'

'We'd rather not make a big thing of this,' said one of the men.

'Big thing, small thing,' said Lorenzo's dad. 'It's a team thing. Lorenzo, round everyone up. We met up with Mamma and the backpacks in two minutes.'

Lorenzo was on his feet. A sharpness in his Dad's voice that said he meant business.

Little Mario hopped up too. 'I'll take the left, you take the right.'

'UG, you stay with me,' said Coach.

Lorenzo's dad turned away from the men and walked with me towards the end of the field. The men followed. He put his arm around my shoulder and said. 'These men are here to talk about our team. They say that this is a boy's league and you're not a boy. I don't think it should matter. But they say that there is a problem because you are a girl. I don't want to decide anything without you and the whole team together. We hear what they have to say, and then we decide. Together. Ok?'

I nodded.

We approached Lorenzo's Mom. Marco was crawling around at her feet. Lorenzo's dad said something to her in Italian. She saw us and gave me a big hug. They talked for a moment.

Soon the team had gathered around.

'Ok,' said Lorenzo's dad to the men in the red jackets. 'Now tell us what the problem is.'

'It's like this,' said the taller of the two men. He had sideburns and thinning hair.

Our small gathering was like a magnet and within moments, a larger group gathered around us. I saw Mr. McCartney and the WildCats' coach join the group.

The man in the red jacket continued. 'This is a boy's league and only boys are allowed to play in the boy's league. That's the rule.'

'What kind of rule is that?' said Lorenzo's dad. 'Isn't this a soccer league? If someone's good at soccer why can't they play?'

'Because this is a boy's league. There is a girl's league and your player can join them. There is some sensitivity to be considered,' said the man.

'Sensitivity?' said Lorenzo's dad. 'Soccer is a game. You run, you pass the ball, you kick the ball, you shoot and score goals. If you have skills, you play. If you don't have skills, you don't ... that's it.'

'But that's not it,' said the shorter man in red. 'There are reasons why we have boys' leagues and girls' leagues.'

'What reasons?' said Lorenzo's dad.

'I'm sorry, coach,' said the taller man. 'We have a tournament to run. We were alerted to the fact that this player is a girl. We could disqualify you from the whole tournament, but we can see that you were unaware of the rules.'

'I know your rules,' said Lorenzo's dad.

But the short man in the red jacket continued, 'you can keep your position as it is, but you are not allowed to have this player on the field for any more matches,' he pointed towards me.

'That's the way it is?'

'Yes,' said both men in red at once.

Mr. McCartney stepped forward. He was dressed in the black and white zebra shirt of a referee. It was clear that other people in the soccer leagues knew who he was. 'For what it's worth,' he said. 'I've seen this player on the field. She is of equal talent and caliber to any other player here, and deserves to play in this tournament. I think it's a shame that this has even come up as an issue.'

The tall man in the red jacket responded. 'We understand. You're a respected coach and referee, but this isn't about talent or ability. It's just that we have rules and we cannot change them today.'

'Ok team,' said Lorenzo's dad. 'Come in.' The boys huddled around him.

I didn't know whether to join in or stand on the side. But Lorenzo's dad reached out an arm gesturing me in.

'You heard these men,' he said. 'I know what I think and what I'd like to do, but I think that we should decide as a team what action we take. We are all in this together.'

'I think it's unfair,' said Lorenzo.

'Me too,' said Little Mario.

'I say if the UG can't play, then I won't play,' said Lorenzo.

'Yeah. Me neither,' said Little Mario.

Aldo chimed in. 'If the UG can't play, then count me out too.'

The two men in the red jackets stepped closer. The shorter one spoke up, 'Coach, you need to make a decision about what your team is going to do because the next round is about to start.'

Lorenzo's dad said, 'I think we should take a vote. The majority rules.'

'NO!' I shouted suddenly.

'It's not fair. We've all been working together to get ready for today. It's not fair if you can't play because of me. If you can't win it with me, then you can win it for me.'

No Way Home

I wanted to run. I wanted to fight. I wanted to kick.

When my teammates and Lorenzo's dad pulled themselves away from me towards the semi-finals, it felt like a bandage was being ripped from my skin.

They had to play. They couldn't give everything up because of me.

But what about me, where could I go? It felt like everyone was looking at me … and laughing. The girl who wanted to look like and play with the boys.

I didn't even know what I was myself anymore.

I wanted to disappear. I wanted to sink into the field.

I decided to run before everyone turned away towards the match and I was completely alone.

Lorenzo's mom held Marco in one arm and was about to put her other arm around me when I ducked and ran.

I ran to the corner of the field, to the fence. I gripped the chain links in my fists as hard as I could. But it didn't hurt enough. I wanted my hands to hurt more and my chest less.

I wanted to bleed so that they could see how much I hurt. 'Girl … Boy … Girl … Boy …' kept pounding in my head.

I heard the ref's whistle and glanced back over my shoulder. The match had started. I stood alone there, separated from the game by the running track and the long jump pit but I felt too exposed. Anyone could turn and see me there. They could see me, but they couldn't see me bleed.

I let go of the fence and ran towards the bleachers that were used for high school football games. I ran up on them to the top. I could see the semi-finals below. It was easy to make out the teams by their colors. I pulled at the collar of my jersey until I could hear the material crackle, ready to rip.

Exposed. Anyone could look up and see me pulling at my shirt.

CRYING … like a girl.

I didn't want to be seen, so I ran down to the back side of the bleachers.

I climbed into the lattice work under them and pulled myself into a ball.

Hidden. Empty. Curled up beside discarded candy wrappers and soda cans and other scrap that had slid down between the cracks.

I cried. I rubbed my head with my fists. I bit into my knees. Snot ran from my nose and mouth. I didn't care. I didn't care about anything.

CRYING … like a boy.

I could hear the others playing in the background. They called to one another. Parents cheered them on.

The ball.

The whistle.

The pounding of their feet on the grass.

I could hear the distance between me and the playing field. The sound of the game was like a bubble, floating away from me.

They had to play. I wanted them to play. I wanted to play. Boy, girl. Whatever.

I'll never play this stupid shit shit shit shit shit shit shit shit shit shit shit shit shit shit shit shit shit shit shit shit shit shit shit game again. Yes, I said SHIT!

'That was about the bravest thing I've ever seen a player do,' said a voice that scared the wits out of me.

I turned and whacked my head on one of the crossbars. It hurt for real.

'You ok?' said Mr. McCartney.

My face was wet with tears and snot. I'd just whacked my bald head. But I nodded … 'yes.'

Mr. McCartney was kneeling in the light. His hand rested on a soccer ball. 'You know,' he said. 'Your team was ready to quit for you. I know that coach Emilio was torn about what to do.'

'I think you did an amazing and noble thing by stepping down just now so that the game could go on,' he said.

'We've been practicing for weeks,' I said. 'All of us. They couldn't quit because of me.'

'You know, Lorenzo, just did the second most noble thing I've seen in a long time.'

'What do you mean?'

'He picked up the ball and stopped play. He told the ref that he would not continue without the whole team. Then he sat down on the field. The rest of the boys also sat where they were. Coach Emilio joined them.'

'Really?'

'Really. They're sitting there now.'

I noticed the difference in sound suddenly. Talking, but no kicking or running, no whistles or cheering.

'I think you're making history,' said Mr. McCartney. 'Maybe you should come out and finish what you've started here.'

I nodded and crawled towards him.

I whacked my head again on the way out. It's easier to hurt yourself when you're not actually trying. Mr. McCartney stood, dropped the ball and popped it up again into my arms. We walked towards the field.

'Can you see that I've been crying?' I asked, wiping my face with my jersey.

'You look fine,' said Mr. McCartney. 'Just fine.'

We approached the field. Parents moved aside to let us pass.

Marco crawled towards me and his mom plucked him up. I walked with Mr. McCartney onto the field.

Then I headed over to Lorenzo.

He looked up at me and said, 'Hey UG.'

'Hey,' I said.

'Have a seat.' He shuffled over.

The Finals

I took my spot beside Lorenzo. The others on my team were sitting down on the field as well. Then the two officials approached Coach Emilio. They spoke in quiet voices. The man with the clipboard's red face looked like it was going to explode. Mr. McCartney joined the officials in the discussion. He was talking calmly but animatedly, the way he talked about history.

Although I couldn't hear what he was saying, I imagined he was giving them a lecture and a list of examples where rules had been bent or broken in tournaments since the days of Sir Lancelot and King Arthur.

I kept one eye on the WildCats' coach. He stood still, gazing out at his players who waited in position opposite us. I didn't know that he had it in him to stand in one place for so long, because every time I'd seen him before, he was pacing and shouting at his team. But then he strode out onto the field. 'I've had enough of this,' he said in a loud voice.

The officials turned their heads. Lorenzo's dad looked shocked, as the WildCats' coach approached the men standing on the opposite side. I thought he might be rushing over to start a fight with Lorenzo's dad.

I was about to jump up and yell, 'STOP! It was a mistake! I shouldn't play, but I am so grateful that my coach and team stood up for me. I'll be ok. I am UG and there is nothing anyone can do about it. Ever again!'

But when the WildCats' coach got to midfield, he stopped in front of his son, who was juggling the ball nervously between his feet and said something to him that I couldn't hear. The boy flipped up the ball, the coach grabbed it, tucked it under his arm and then plopped himself down straight across the centerline from where Lorenzo and I were sitting. He nodded over to me. Then his son sat down next to his father and, one by one, the rest of their team followed.

Seeing this, Lorenzo's dad left the discussion with the officials and came to sit down beside the WildCats' coach. The two men nodded to one another, smiling.

Mr. McCartney had finished his discourse and came over to sit beside the two coaches. The two officials were still standing on the sidelines.

Pietro's Dad left the small row of bleachers where the parents were standing and crossed the field to sit beside the other men. He smiled at me and nodded to Pietro. I remembered his fantastic gift of the amazing pizza and cannoli. The twenty dollars were now burning a hole in my gym bag.

The two officials approached the men sitting in the field.

The talkative one spoke, 'we're going to have to cancel this match if you don't begin to play.'

'We can't have a draw in a competition,' said the other. 'According to the rules there has to be a winner.'

'I suggest we play for it,' said Lorenzo's dad.

The two officials stared down at him.

'It's the only way,' said the Wild Cats' coach. 'When we beat this team, we want to beat the whole team.'

'I give up!' Shouted the talkative official. He handed his clipboard and his whistle to the other and stomped off the field.

'Allora…Let's play some football,' said Lorenzo's dad. He was already on his feet and stretched out a hand to the WildCats' coach. 'Grazie.'

'You won't be thanking me when we crush you,' said the WildCats' coach. He trotted towards the sidelines tossing the ball to one of his sons. 'Don't lose this,' he said.

'No way, Dad,' said the boy.

I'd learnt a lot over the last few months, but as soon as the game started, it felt like it had all disappeared. I was so used to fighting, and this was the first time that anyone had ever stood up for me. I didn't know what to do. I just wanted to let the WildCats win and go eat pizza. I wanted the match to end.

But then, the push was on. Their forward passed the ball to his right and I was in play. Defense. As he whizzed past me I came to my senses.

'UG! Defense!' Shouted Coach.

I nearly stuck out my leg for an illegal tackle, but instead, I circled down field and tried to catch up. He was quick and got ahead of me. I had to count on one of our backs to take over. I ran center and hoped to pick off his pass. I was lucky when Aldo shut the boy down and he passed back. I intercepted the ball and kicked it across the field to Pietro, who lobbed it to Lorenzo running up center.

Our first try. I ran full steam up the left hand side of the field. Lorenzo passed their midfield and gunned it down center.

He passed back to Pietro, who controlled the ball and kicked it hard towards Lorenzo, who couldn't make it in time to intercept the pass.

I ran to the corner and stopped the ball just before it went out. Then I improvised a corner kick to the middle with Lorenzo center and Pietro on the right.

The pass curved upwards. Lorenzo missed the header. The ball bounced in front of Pietro. It was moving fast but he got a foot on it. Jumped up and shot. Goal!

My heart was pumping so fast that I nearly keeled over.

The Wild Cats' coach shouted at his team. 'What are you doing out there! You play like a bunch of GIRLS!'

'You wish,' I said louder than I meant to.

An Empty Goal

A week had passed since the tournament, and Mom hadn't said a word about it. I waited in my room until my brothers were out of the house. I could hear them in the backyard, arguing over basketball. It was a good time to have breakfast in peace. And then I'd slip out to Lorenzo's house. We were working hard on our school presentation.

'Morning,' I said to Mom.

She looked up from the television and sipped her coffee. I stopped for a moment in front of her, studying the folds in her off–pink bathrobe.

I was about to head into the kitchen for a blueberry breakfast.

'I heard you did good last week,' she said.

'Yeah,' I said.

She took a slurp of her coffee and in the pause, I could hear them outside. 'Out on you! You get it! No, You get it! You touched it last!'

'I just can't take the fighting,' she said.

'I'm not fighting,' I said. But I was ready to fight. Ready to run out. Ready to scream. Ready to kick … if I had to.

'I'm sorry,' she said, placing her cup on the coffee table.

I knelt on the shaggy orange carpet and she slipped off the couch. I let her hug me.

'I'm sorry,' she whispered.

She reached out and rubbed her hands over my bald head.

'It suits you,' she said.

'Thanks,' I said. 'Well … Lorenzo's expecting me, Mom. I should have breakfast.'

'Ok,' she rolled herself back up onto the couch.

I could feel her watching me as I retrieved the blueberries from the freezer and poured milk on them.

She lifted her coffee, stood up, walked towards the kitchen and sat across from me at the table.

She sipped from her cup and I ate up as quickly as I could.

'You're nothing like me,' she said. 'You're so … independent.'

'Yeah,' I said. 'I guess.' I slurped down the bright blue milk.

'If I were more like you, things would have been different. I wouldn't have waited so long.'

'Waited for what?' I asked.

'Everything,' she said. 'I've been waiting for everything my whole life. Waiting for my ship to come in. Waiting for something good to happen. Waiting for the fighting to end. Waiting to be rescued by my prince in shining armor.'

She rocked her head from side to side like a Bollywood actress. For a moment, she looked pretty, like she did when she was happy. She was pretty when she was younger, even though most of the pictures were in faded Polaroid.

Coach says, 'you have to meet the ball. If you wait for a pass, you'll miss it. If you see a shot, you have to take it. If you wait, you'll lose the chance. And if you wait for an empty goal, forget it.'

'I was thinking that maybe I could come see you play some time.'

'Ok,' I said.

'Maybe your next match?'

'Sure,' I said. 'Anyway, I should head off soon. Lorenzo's expecting me.'

I rinsed my bowl in the sink and grabbed my gym bag. 'Bye, Mom.'

'Bye, UG.'

I turned. It was the first time she said it. 'See you when I get back.'

The Beautiful Game

I was more nervous standing in front of the class beside Lorenzo than
I had ever felt running next to him on the football field. Mr. McCartney
leaned against the wall at the back of the room waiting for us to begin.

We had run through our presentation a few times at home. Lorenzo's
parents acted as our audience. They had actually bought me the Brazilian
number 10 jersey that I was wearing. Pelé's number. Even though I wasn't
a striker, it felt right to wear it.

I stood, holding the ball in my hands like a giant slippery watermelon.
It felt heavy. My mouth was dry. I glanced over at Lorenzo, who was
staring at the floor.

'Ummmm,' I mumbled.

Blank.

I totally forgot what I was going to say.

The official FIFA World Cup ball I was holding doubled, tripled,
quadrupled in weight. It dropped to the floor.

PANIC! My hands ran with sweat.

Then, my soccer training kicked in.

I tapped up lightly on the bottom of the ball and it snapped to up to waist height. Once, twice, three times. Then I juggled it up to my knee.

I glanced over at Mr. McCartney, thinking he'll be really mad, but NO. He was smiling and he nodded. 'Yes.'

I juggled the ball between my knees, back and forth. The rhythm of the juggling seemed to awaken Lorenzo and he looked up at me. My teammate, my best friend … ready.

I popped the ball up and knocked it with the side of my head and Lorenzo tapped it back. We headed the ball back and forth a few times and then he caught the ball on the top of his neck, widening his shoulders. He flipped it up with his head and it sailed in an arch.

The class roared with applause as I let it travel the whole distance to my foot, catching it and holding it with my ankle. Then I flipped it up to Lorenzo who juggled it rapidly, a few times. He popped it up and spun his body around like a street dancer and kept juggling. He spun again and kept juggling.

Such a show off! I wish I could have done that. I was good, but not that good. At least not yet!

The class clapped loudly. He did a spin and a half and bopped the ball over to me with his butt. The class burst into laughter and applause.

I kneed it up to head height and then bounced it on my head with a lighter and lighter touch until it was resting on my forehead and I moved to keep balance like a seal does balancing a ball on its snout at the aquarium. This was my best trick. The applause grew the longer I kept it up. At first, they clapped normally, and then together in a rhythm. The attention started to make me blush and lose my concentration. Finally, I had to pop it up and head it over to Lorenzo. He controlled the ball first with his feet.

Tap, tap, tap, tap, tap.

He finished by kicking the ball up again and letting it fall behind him. He popped it up with the back of his foot at the last moment. It arched back over his head and I caught it.

My hands were dry.

'Soccer,' I said. 'Football. Calcio...'

I talked about the history of the game. 'Ball sports have existed for thousands of years in Egypt, Ancient China, and through the Middle Ages in what was now England. It evolved through time until 1863 when twelve London clubs got together and formed the Football Association. They wrote down the rules of the game to separate Rugby Football from Association Football.'

'You may wonder why soccer is called football in some places and soccer in others,' said Lorenzo.

'Well, I'll tell you,' I said, remembering how we had practiced our routine. 'When the Football Association was formed, people in England called rugby football 'Ruggers Football' and association football 'Assoccer' ... short for association. Then students dropped the 'a' to make it shorter and just called it soccer. I suppose they were just as lazy as we are.

'After a while, football became so popular in England that people just used the word football ... but by the time it came to the US, Football in America was a completely different game, so they used the old name for the game ... Soccer.'

'In Italy, they use the word *calcio* which means 'kick ball,' said Lorenzo because when the sport came to Italy in the 1800s that's how people translated it.'

We talked about the different positions and I had a diagram that I drew with all of the different names, so that people could see how the team had to work together to win.

'Soccer is about creating a team with players who have different strengths. They use passing and positioning to create opportunities to make goals. It's a game of strategy and timing. But mostly it's a game of passion. There's a reason why soccer, football …'

'*Calcio,*' said Lorenzo right on cue.

'… Is the most popular sport in the world. Anyone can play it. All you need is a ball. And if you play great soccer … like Pelé said, it's a Beautiful Game.'

GC Fabbri was raised on his grandmother's stories. She'd send him, his brother, sister and a group of his cousins on worldwide adventures. One day they would join the circus and another fly around the world in a hot air balloon.

One time he managed to save the Golden Gate Bridge from collapse with an indestructible shoelace. Another time, he travelled to Africa to assist local park rangers protecting the nearly extinct black rhinoceros from a group of evil poachers.

Grandma lived in a tiny cabin on the edge of a small town by a lake with a dog, Jeffry, two cats, and a large calico duck who liked nothing better than to steal Jeffry's crunchy dog nuggets from a bowl on the back porch. When she wasn't telling stories, she cooked and listened to the radio.

He still remembers his grandmother's voice when he sits down in the early morning in his Stockholm studio to write his own stories.

The combination of writing and illustration keeps him inspired because there's always something new to learn and explore.

When he's not writing or painting, you can find him out playing soccer with his two boys Maxi and Ruben, cooking or jogging around the nearby lake.

www.ingramcontent.com/pod-product-compliance
Lightning Source LLC
Chambersburg PA
CBHW021405150726
47989CB00005B/2409